"I know you for what you are."

Arden moved quickly, but not quickly enough. Conor caught hold of her wrist before she could strike him.

"Don't," he said, very softly. "Not unless you're prepared to face the consequences."

She stood facing him, her face white, her eyes brimming with unshed tears. Her voice trembled when she spoke. "I hate you!" she said.

He laughed. "What has that to do with anything?"

Her brain worked desperately for words that would tell him how despicable he was, but before she could think of anything, he cupped the back of her head, drew her toward him and ⬤⬤⬤⬤ ⬤⬤ hard on the mouth.

"I won't buy you⬤⬤⬤⬤⬤⬤⬤⬤⬤⬤⬤⬤⬤⬤ his thumb ove⬤⬤⬤⬤⬤⬤⬤⬤⬤⬤⬤⬤ patient man. I ⬤⬤⬤⬤⬤⬤⬤⬤⬤⬤⬤⬤ way to my bed on you⬤⬤⬤⬤⬤⬤

SANDRA MARTON is the author of more than thirty romance novels. Readers around the world love her strong, passionate heroes and determined, spirited heroines. When she's not writing, Sandra likes to hike, read, explore out-of-the-way restaurants and travel to faraway places. The mother of two grown sons, Sandra lives with her husband in a sun-filled house in a quiet corner of Connecticut where she alternates between extravagant bouts of gourmet cooking and take-out pizza. Sandra loves to hear from her readers. You can write to her (SASE) at P.O. Box 295, Storrs, Connecticut 06268.

Coming in 1998!

Three brides, three grooms—

and they all meet at the **Wedding of the Year.**

Look our for Sandra Marton's memorable new series

in Harlequin Presents.

"Extraordinary tension, exceptional scenes...larger than life characters who will walk off the pages and into your heart."—*Romantic Times*

SANDRA MARTON

Master of El Corazon

Harlequin Books

TORONTO • NEW YORK • LONDON
AMSTERDAM • PARIS • SYDNEY • HAMBURG
STOCKHOLM • ATHENS • TOKYO • MILAN
MADRID • WARSAW • BUDAPEST • AUCKLAND

ISBN 0-373-11928-3

MASTER OF EL CORAZON

First North American Publication 1997.

Copyright © 1994 by Sandra Myles.

CHAPTER ONE

THE night the world came tumbling down around Arden Miller's ears began just like any other, or, at least, like any other during the five months since she'd transferred from McCann, Flint, Emerson's New York office to the firm's newest branch in Costa Rica.

She put in her usual eight hours as executive secretary to Edgar Lithgow, bid him a polite good evening, then drove her Ford Escort—a perk of her new job—the few miles to the hotel in which the company housed its small roster of North American employees.

The clerk at the reception desk greeted her pleasantly.

'*Buenas noches, señorita.* The cook says to tell you the *langosta* is especially good tonight.'

Arden smiled. 'I'm sure it is, but I think I'll settle for a chicken sandwich in my room. Would you ask Alejandro to bring it up in an hour or so?'

The clerk smiled. 'With iced coffee, yes?'

'Please.'

'Of course, Señorita Miller. It will be my pleasure.'

No, Arden thought, no, all of this is *my* pleasure. I have never been so fussed over, or made to feel so much at home as I have these last months.

But she didn't say that, of course. Such an admission would have been far too personal and out of keeping with her carefully honed professional image. Instead she gave him another smile, scooped up the few messages and letters that had been left for her, and made her way to the lift. She stabbed the button, then turned her attention to the envelopes in her hand.

There was an advertisement from Macy's, urging her
to take advantage of a sale on shoes, and a form letter
from a candidate for local office, pleading for her vote
in an election that had taken place a month before. Arden
smiled. It was amazing, the mail the post office re-routed
so it followed you all these thousands of miles.

The third letter was from her mother, and Arden
opened it eagerly. Evelyn wrote that she was feeling fine
and still happy in her new job as live-in housekeeper to
the Carsons, up on the Hill in Greenfield. Did Arden
remember them? Arden's mouth turned down. Yes, she
certainly did. They'd had a couple of sons who'd thought
it was their absolute right to sexually initiate girls from
the Valley in the back seats of their cars, and if there
were any complaints they'd had the money and the clout
to hush them up.

Her gaze dropped to the next paragraph. There was
good news about Emma Simms, her mother said. She'd
just finished a course in beauty school and she was head
over heels in love with that nice Evans boy, the one who
was working over at Destry's Plumbing. They planned
to get married in February and honeymoon in
Disneyworld. And Nan Richards was pregnant with her
third baby and working weekends for a caterer so she
and her husband could buy a house.

Arden shook her head. Some things never changed,
nor did the expectations of some people. She loved her
mother dearly, but how Evelyn could be content working
as a servant for the rich was beyond her to understand.
As for the news about the girls she'd grown up with—
well, if Emma and Nan were happy, that was wonderful,
but for Arden happiness had always meant establishing
herself in a career. You had to have goals in life, and
the higher, the better.

As for falling head over heels in love and getting married—well, that sort of nonsense made for catchy song titles, but it had little place in——

'Señorita.'

Arden's head lifted sharply. The lift had arrived, the door had slid open, and she saw that a man was lounging in the far corner, watching her. His arms were folded across his chest, his feet were crossed at the ankle, and he had a lazy smile on his beard-stubbled face.

His eyes—surprisingly green in his sun-darkened face—met hers, and she took an unexpected step back. For barely an instant she'd felt—she'd felt as if the ground had suddenly tilted under her feet . . .

She gave herself a mental shake. That was what came of skipping lunch. But Mr Lithgow had asked her if she'd mind working through, so she could finish up the reports he'd needed for an afternoon meeting——

'Espera usted a alguine?'

She looked at the man again. Are you waiting for someone? he'd asked, his husky voice and little smile adding a twist to the simple words so that she knew he was asking more than the reason she hadn't yet stepped into the lift. The knowledge made her hazel eyes turn cool.

Did he really think she could possibly be interested in someone like him? Yes, she thought, her mouth tightening with distaste, he probably did. He had to know there were women—lots of women—who'd look at such a man and like what they saw. He was tall, wide in the shoulders and narrow in the hips, with a classically handsome Spanish face that was made even more attractive by a nose that seemed to have been broken some time in the past. A canvas backpack leaned against his leg, its age and condition matched by his dusty leather boots. He wore jeans and a denim work shirt with the sleeves rolled back to show tanned, muscular forearms.

But any woman with half a brain would see beyond the blatantly macho good looks. Arden had seen others like him several times since she'd arrived in San José, the sort of man who'd come to Central America from any of a dozen other places with nothing but a passport and a handful of *colones* in his pocket. Some people called them adventurers, but what was the sense in using romantic euphemisms to cover the truth? He was a tramp and a drifter, a man who never planned beyond tomorrow and earned what money he needed by signing on for a day's manual labour here and there in his travels. Heaven only knew how he'd scraped together enough to rent a room here for the night.

'*Que pasa, señorita?*'

'*No me interesa,*' she said, her voice cutting sharply across his.

His smile tilted. 'Ah,' he said in unaccented English, 'you are North American, not a Tica.'

'That's right, I'm not Costa Rican.' Why did it irk her that her accent had given her away, despite her excellent command of the language? 'And I'm not——'

'Interested. Yes, so you said.' His gaze moved over her in frank appraisal and he smiled lazily. 'But you misunderstood me, *señorita*. It's not that I mind waiting. You're worth it. A pretty woman always is. It's just that a lift's whole purpose is to go up, and this one hasn't moved for the past five minutes.'

It took her a moment before she understood that he'd somehow turned the tables on her. Of course he'd been coming on to her; you didn't have to be interested in such ridiculous games in order to know when you'd been invited to play. But she'd made him feel foolish by putting him down and now he was repaying her in kind.

Arden's eyes narrowed. She wanted to tell him that as far as she was concerned, he could have the damned lift all to himself for the rest of the evening, if he wanted it, but she knew it was more important to show no reaction.

'Sorry,' she said with a cool smile.

She stepped into the car and turned her back to him. The door slid shut and the lift jerked to a start. It rose slowly, as it always did, although this evening it seemed to be taking forever to make the journey to the third floor. She could feel the man's eyes on her, burning a hole in her back. After a moment, he cleared his throat.

'Are you new to Costa Rica?' he said pleasantly.

Arden rolled her eyes to the ceiling. He was going to try again! Well, she wasn't going to be drawn in this time. Her chin lifted; she stared at the door as if she expected to see a message flash on the dark wood.

'Because, if you are,' he said, 'I'd be more than happy to——'

Lord, he was persistent! 'Thank you,' she said in a voice that would have turned warm water to ice, 'but I'm busy.'

'—buy you a drink and tell you a bit about——'

She swung towards him, and her voice grew even more frigid. 'I said I'm busy.'

'There's a cocktail party this evening, beside the pool. Just give me half an hour to shower and change,' he said, as if she hadn't spoken. His hand lifted, went to his face, and he rubbed his knuckles lightly over the dark stubble that covered his chin. 'And to shave, of course,' he said with a smile. 'I've been in the back country for days, and——'

How would the faint roughness of his beard feel against her skin? The question sprang into her mind with no warning at all. A flush rose in her cheeks and she swung away and jabbed her finger at the floor button, trying futilely to speed the lift's sloth-like progress.

'You're wasting your time,' she said, her anger at herself and at him making her voice hard-edged and brittle. 'I'm sure this town's full of women who'll be delighted by your story, but I'm not one of them.'

He chuckled softly, as if she'd said something amusing instead of insulting. 'Tales of the jungle don't turn you on?'

'If you mean,' she said, giving him a look of absolute distaste, 'do I think there's charm to being a bum, the answer is no, I do not.'

Her sharp words had the desired effect this time. His eyes narrowed, and the smiling, handsome face took on a look of coldness.

'Your honesty does you credit, *señorita.*'

'Yes,' Arden said, just as coldly, 'I've been told that before.'

The lift jogged to a stop. Finally! she thought, and she stepped briskly into the hall. After a second or two, the man's footsteps followed after her. Arden gritted her teeth. He wasn't just persistent, he was impossible! She took a deep breath and spun around to face him. 'Listen here,' she said fiercely, 'if you think——'

Her words sputtered to silence. The stranger wasn't following her, he was unlocking the door to what was obviously his room. He looked up, and his eyes, as green and cold as those of a jungle cat, met hers.

'*Adios, señorita.* Don't think it's been charming, because it hasn't.'

Arden's mouth dropped open. She wanted to make a sharp, clever rejoinder, but her mind was a blank. Instead, she tossed her head, turned on her heel, and strode down the corridor to her room. She stabbed her

key into the lock, shoved the door open, then slammed
it after her.

Before you knew it, this hotel would be renting rooms
to just about anybody!

She marched stiffly through her small sitting-room to
the bedroom and tossed her key on the table. After a
moment, she sighed and sank into a chair. There was
no reason to let such a silly encounter upset her. She'd
had a long, hard day, she'd been looking forward to a
relaxing evening, and she certainly wasn't going to let a
run-in with an arrogant fool snatch that away from her!

She kicked off her beige pumps, stretched out her legs,
and began leafing through the remaining messages still
clutched in her hand.

There was one from Julie Squires, the newest New
York transfer. Would Arden like to take the train ride
to Limon on Saturday? Arden sighed again. Sure, she
would, even though she'd already made the near
obligatory trip to the coastal town. Julie was feeling dis-
placed, something Arden understood all too well. Costa
Rica was beautiful and the people were warm and
friendly, but it was hard not to feel at a loose end your
first few weeks.

The second message was from the hotel, a gaily
coloured flyer reminding guests of tonight's poolside
party. Arden rose to her feet, stripped off her suit jacket,
and tossed it across a chair. The Lift Lothario would
certainly be in attendance, but she would not.

Not that she'd ever had any intention of attending,
she thought as she unzipped her skirt and stepped out
of it. She'd never liked parties, always felt self-conscious
at them, half waiting for another guest to point a finger
at her and ask people *who* had invited *her*?

Arden smiled a bit grimly as she peeled off her blouse
and underwear and dropped them on the chair. And it

didn't take a psychologist to figure out that little scenario, she thought as she padded into the bathroom and turned on the shower. When you spent your teenage years passing hors-d'oeuvres and drinks to people you saw every day, you could easily end up with a very different attitude about partygoing.

'It's an easy way to make a little extra money,' her mother had always said when she pressed Arden into serving at weekends at the Potts mansion where she'd worked as a maid, and Arden would never have hurt her by arguing, but the truth was that it was a terrible way to earn money, wearing a black uniform with a tiny white apron and trying not to react when kids from your English or mathematics classes looked straight through you as if they'd never seen you before.

Actually, she thought as she pinned her dark auburn hair into a top knot and stepped under the shower, she had gone to one of the hotel's parties a couple of months ago, after her boss had urged her to do so for weeks.

'It's simply an act of sociability, Miss Miller,' Mr Lithgow had said crisply. 'I have no interest in such non-sense either, but the New York office has made a special point of asking us all to do our part in being friendly to the Costa Ricans.'

Arden had thought that being friendly to a bunch of hotel guests hardly qualified, but she'd kept her opinion to herself. Edgar Lithgow had selected her for this job personally, choosing her instead of two other equally qualified applicants because, he'd said sternly, he knew he could count on her to put the interests of the firm before her own, and she wasn't about to give him reason to think otherwise.

And so, with great reluctance, she'd agreed to go to the party. But she'd felt even more out of place than usual, in the midst of vacationers partying at an almost

frantic pace while she'd stood there in a grey business
suit, trying to look at ease, and not even Mr Lithgow's
attempts at sociability had helped. In fact, Arden
thought, wincing at the memory, she'd been so stiff and
uncomfortable that she'd almost made a damned fool
of herself when her boss had come striding towards her
with two tall, frosted glasses in his hands.

'No, thank you, sir,' she'd said, when he'd held one
of the glasses out to her.

'Don't be silly, Miss Miller,' he'd said with a frown.
'It's only punch.'

And so she'd taken the glass, then a sip from it, just
to be polite. It hadn't tasted bad at all, sort of fruity
and cool and sweet, but there must have been enough
rum in it to have gone straight to her head because moments later, she'd imagined Mr Lithgow looking at her
in a way he never had before, with a sharp brightness
glinting in the pale blue eyes behind their tri-focal lenses,
and then she'd thought he'd moved closer to her than
he had to, so that his arm kept brushing against her breast
each time he lifted his glass.

But the final moment of foolishness had come when
she felt his hand settle on her hip, the fingers lightly
cupping her buttocks. Arden still shuddered when she
thought of it.

'Mr Lithgow,' she'd said, loudly and sharply enough
to have made a couple of heads turn in their direction,
but before she could make a complete ass of herself,
thank God, her boss had frowned and nodded towards
the pool and said that it was a good thing he'd grabbed
her in time or the jostling crowd would have tumbled
her straight in. Arden had blushed with embarrassment
at what she'd been thinking, claimed a headache, and
fled to her rooms where she'd reminded herself that one
of the reasons she'd accepted this transfer was not just

because it could well lead to a promotion but because
Edgar Lithgow, while rich, was as harmless as a dodo.
He had a wife, five children, a paunch and a shiny scalp,
and he was on the board of half a dozen religious and
charitable organisations.

Arden turned off the shower and stepped from the
tub. In five months here, she thought as she wrapped
herself in a floor-length towelling robe, working side by
side all day, bumping into each other with regularity in
the hotel dining-room or reading lounge in the evening,
he had never given her the slightest reason to find fault
with him. In fact, she doubted he'd ever really noticed
if she were male or female. She shuddered as she un-
pinned her hair, then combed it out until it lay in darkly
curling abundance on her shoulders.

'Thank your lucky stars you didn't make a fool of
yourself that night, Arden,' she whispered to her reflection in the misted mirror. The last thing she wanted was
to lose this job and the chance it offered of a better
future.

There was a knock at the door to her suite. Had an
hour gone by already? Not that it mattered; she'd eat
just as she was, in her robe at the little table by the
window in the sitting-room, and then she'd curl up in
bed with the book she'd started last evening.

The knock came again, just as she reached the door
and unlocked it.

'*Buenas noches, Alejandro,*' she said—and stared in
surprise.

It was not the bellman with her dinner tray who stood
in the hallway.

It was her boss, Edgar Lithgow.

CHAPTER TWO

ARDEN tried not to cringe as Lithgow's gaze swept over her, all the way from her damp, tousled hair to her bare toes peeking out from under her robe. He frowned and she moaned inwardly. She looked about as unprofessional as it was possible to look—but then, she certainly hadn't expected a visitor! With difficulty, she managed what she hoped might pass for a polite smile.

'Mr Lithgow, sir. What a surprise.'

'Good evening, Miss Miller. I apologise for the intrusion, but something's come up, and I wondered if I might bother you to take a short memo.'

'Now?' she said stupidly.

He frowned again. 'I know it's irregular and I apologise. But it will only take a moment, I promise.'

Arden stared at him. It was, indeed, irregular. Until this instant, she'd never even seen him on her floor.

'Miss Miller?'

Her hesitation had turned Lithgow's frown into a scowl. She gave him one more quick glance, as if to reassure herself that he were the same man she worked with each day, tall and angular in a dark blue suit, his few strands of pale hair combed neatly across his skull, his rimless eye glasses perched high on his narrow nose, and then she smiled.

'Of course,' she said, opening the door wide. 'Come in.'

Lithgow stepped past her into the room, and her nose wrinkled. He'd brought a scent with him—what was it?

15

Cologne? Shaving lotion? She'd never noticed him wearing either.

Gin, Arden thought in surprise. Was that what she smelled? Gin?

'Your notepad, Miss Miller. Where is it?'

She hesitated. 'It's—it's——'

'This is quite an urgent memo, Miss Miller. I'd prefer not to waste time standing around this way.' He turned and slammed the door shut. 'And I've no wish to have anyone hear me dictate something of such importance.'

Arden glanced at the closed door, then at her boss's face. He looked as he always did, coldly forbidding and somewhat unapproachable.

'Miss Miller?' His voice was sharp. 'Is there a problem?'

'No.' She shook her head. 'No, sir, of course not.'

Not unless you called her own silly imagination a problem, Arden thought. The run-in with the stranger had obviously made her edgy, and foolishly so. If Edgar Lithgow wanted to have a drink on his own time, that was his business. If he needed to dictate an urgent memo, that was hers, and never mind that she wasn't really comfortable having him turn up in her rooms after working hours.

'I have some stationery in the dresser in the bedroom,' she said as she started from the room. 'I'll just get it and——'

'You weren't at the party, Miss Miller.'

Arden turned in surprise. Lithgow had followed her; he was almost on her heels and now that he was so close to her, the smell of gin was strong enough to make her wrinkle her nose.

'Uh, no, no, I wasn't.' She glanced down at herself and flushed, which was silly, considering that she was covered from throat to toe. Still, if she was going to take dictation, she suddenly wanted to change from her robe to something more substantial. 'I—uh—I was just taking a shower,' she said with a quick smile. 'Why don't you go back into the sitting-room and give me a minute to put on——?'

'Don't be silly, Miss Miller.' He smiled. 'Stay just as you are, my dear. You look quite comfortable.'

My dear? Arden cleared her throat. She wanted to take a step back, but the bed was just behind her, pressing lightly against the backs of her legs. 'Well, then,' she said briskly, 'let me just get that paper and we'll get started.'

'By all means.'

'You'll—you'll have to move, sir.' His brows rose questioningly. 'The paper's over there,' she said, gesturing towards the dresser on the far wall. 'I need to get past you.'

Lithgow smiled and shifted slightly to the side. 'You're a slender girl, Arden. Surely you don't need more room than this?'

All at once, everything in the room seemed slightly askew, like a scene viewed through a pair of unfocused binoculars. Be calm, she told herself, just take things nice and easy.

'You know, Mr Lithgow,' she said with a careful smile, 'it really is very late. Alejandro will be bringing my supper in a moment, and——'

Lithgow chuckled slyly. 'No, he won't.'

Arden stared at him. 'What do you mean?'

'I met Alejandro in the hall and told him you and I would prefer a little supper served later, not now.'

'You had no right to do that,' Arden said sharply. She pushed past Lithgow, trying not to notice the press of his body against hers. 'I think you'd better leave right now, sir. If you do——'

Lithgow caught hold of her wrist. 'I haven't dictated the memo yet, Arden.'

'You can dictate it tomorrow, at the office.'

He looked at her steadily, while she tried not to let her growing fear show in her face, and then he sighed and let go of her hand.

'You're right, I should never have bothered you with such nonsense this evening.'

The breath whooshed from her lungs. 'That's all right, sir,' she said. 'We'll—we'll just forget all about——'

'Do you think I might have a cold drink, before I go?'

No, Arden thought, no, you can't. Just get out of here and let me pretend this never happened.

'Miss Miller?' She looked at him. 'I would be most grateful for just a little sip of something cold.'

She sighed. 'Very well, sir. I'll get you a glass of water.'

He shuddered. 'That bottled stuff? No, I don't care for the taste.' He nodded towards the little fridge the hotel provided. 'What do you have in there?'

'Coke and some orange juice,' she said reluctantly, 'but—— '

'And ice?'

All right, she told herself, all right, if that was what it took to get rid of him...

'Yes,' she said with a sigh, 'of course.' She bent and opened the fridge. 'Which would you like, sir? Coke? Or——'

'Just the ice, Arden,' he said, and it was the tone of his voice as much as the way he'd gone back to using her first name that made her look up. That sly grin was on his face again and, as she watched, he pulled a bottle of gin from his pocket. 'Ta da!' he said. 'If Arden won't come to the party, the party will come to her!'

Arden straightened up slowly. 'You'll have to leave now, Mr Lithgow.'

'I agree with you, my dear. Business can wait until morning.' He smiled again. 'Why don't you get us some glasses, hmm?'

'Mr Lithgow——'

'Edgar.'

'Mr Lithgow,' she said firmly, 'you're going to regret this tomorrow. Now, why don't you——?'

'What I regret,' he said, moving towards her, 'is all the time I've wasted, watching you slip around the office, waggling your hips in my face, showing off those breasts, and not doing what a man ought to do when faced with what was offered.'

Arden's hazel eyes widened. 'That's a lie! I never——'

'Temptation was put in my path,' he said solemnly, putting the gin bottle on the night stand as he walked slowly towards her, 'and for months I thought it was a test of my virtue.' He laughed softly. 'And then I realised that I'd misunderstood. You weren't here to tempt me, you were a gift.'

'Now, wait just a damned minute,' Arden said, moving backwards.

'A gift from my maker, Arden.' He was standing almost on top of her now; his breath was a cloud of gin, rising like an evil miasma to her nostrils. 'His way of thanking me for my years of dedication to charitable works.'

He's crazy, Arden thought frantically. Either that, or he's suddenly developed a sick sense of humour. But the hot weight of his hand at her breast was no joke. Arden skidded away.

'Get out of my room,' she said, hoping he could not hear the fear in her voice.

His face took on a look of cold calculation. 'You forget yourself. I have a perfect right to be here. I pay the bills for this suite, remember?'

'The company pays the bills.'

'A matter of semantics.'

'This is sexual harassment,' Arden said quickly. 'You must know there are laws against this sort of——'

'Laws!' Lithgow laughed. 'Stuff and nonsense, pushed through American courts by damned fool feminists. But we're not in America now, we're in a place that looks like Paradise.'

It was no time to argue that the laws still applied, Arden thought desperately. He was either crazy or crazy drunk, and all that mattered was getting away from him while she still could. She looked past him to the door, measuring the distance, wondering if she could reach it before he did, but before there was time to make a move Lithgow lunged for her and grabbed her. Arden cried out and struggled to free herself, but he was a man with a strength fuelled by equal parts desire and alcohol.

'You son of a bitch,' she panted, and somehow she wrenched free, but Lithgow was still holding on to her sash so that the robe swung open, revealing her.

He moaned as if he'd just seen the Grail.

'Lovely,' he said, and the huskiness of that one word told her this would be her last chance at escape.

Arden gave a sob, spun around and raced not for the door but for the night table. The gin bottle crashed to the floor as she reached for the phone, but her fingers closed around thin air. Lithgow grunted, tackled her from behind, and they fell to bed together in a whirl of legs and arms while the stink of gin filled the air in the bedroom.

'Little wildcat,' he said, grinning into her face.

She fought as he tried to pin her beneath him. 'Let go of me, you bastard,' she panted. Her leg came up; she wanted to knee him in the groin but he moved suddenly, feinting to the side. Arden opened her mouth to scream and Lithgow's lips clamped on to hers. The vile taste of him made her gag. She beat against his shoulders, the breath whistling through her nostrils, and suddenly she heard the door slam against the wall and a male voice said, 'Just what in hell is going on here?'

Lithgow went still as a corpse above her. 'Get off me,' Arden said in a voice that shook, as much with rage as with fear. The pupils in his eyes contracted, his mouth narrowed, and suddenly he was Edgar Lithgow again, cool and removed and as proper as a Sunday afternoon in the country.

He rose to his feet and Arden scrambled off the bed in one swift motion, turning to her saviour with a tremulous smile of relief.

'Thank you,' she murmured. 'You got here just in——'

The words caught in her throat. The man standing in the bedroom doorway was the man she'd met in the lift, and he was looking at her as if she'd just climbed out from under a rock.

'It would seem you were telling the truth when you said you had a prior engagement this evening,' he said with a cool smile.

Arden felt a crimson flush rise beneath her skin. 'I'd hardly call this a prior engagement,' she said stiffly.

His gaze was slow and insolent as it skimmed her tangled hair and flushed face, then dropped lower. Her flush deepened as she realised her robe was still hanging open, and she grasped the lapels quickly and drew them tightly together. He looked away from her, his glance moving around the room, and Arden's eyes followed his, taking in, as he was, the tangled bedclothes, her clothing lying carelessly across the chair. When his nostrils flared, hers did, too, and filled with the heavy aroma of gin.

'What would you call it, *señorita*?' he asked, his face expressionless.

Arden grabbed her sash and knotted it tightly at her waist. 'My God,' she said, 'anyone with half a brain can see what——'

'An excellent question, sir.' Arden and the stranger both turned and looked at Edgar Lithgow. He was standing beside the bed, his thin mouth narrowed with disgust, his hair smoothed down across his head, his shirt tucked neatly into his trousers, looking as out of place as a robed jurist in a prison cell. 'Perhaps she'll explain this little scene to us both.'

Arden stared at him. 'What are you talking about?' she said angrily.

Lithgow's eyes never left the other man's face. 'This young woman—Miss Miller—has been my secretary for months now, and in all that time I've chosen to ignore the hints she's given me as to her baser nature.'

'What?' Arden slammed her hands on to her hips. 'What are you saying, you—you——?'

'I'm a family man, sir, a devoted husband and father, a leader in my church and community.' Lithgow shook his head. 'Perhaps that's why I gave Miss Miller the benefit of the doubt, why I pretended not to notice the way she brushed against me whenever she could. But tonight, when she invited me to her room——'

'It's a lie! I never——'

'We had a drink together,' Lithgow said. He sighed. 'More than one, to be honest. And I weakened, heaven forgive me, and she—she——'

'You bastard!' Arden started towards him, but the stranger stopped her, reaching out and catching her by the arm. 'He's lying,' she said furiously. 'I never asked him here, and I certainly never offered him a drink.' She swung towards Lithgow, her eyes flashing. 'You—you forced yourself on me, you pig!'

The stranger let go of her, laughed softly, and leaned back against the door, his hands shoved lazily into his pockets. He had shaved, Arden noticed in some still-logical part of her mind, and changed from his worn denims to a pair of white duck trousers and a pale blue shirt.

'A modern-day version of *Rashomon*,' he said. 'The Japanese play—do you know it? A woman claims rape, a man claims seduction, and it's up to the audience to determine the truth.'

Colour leaped into Arden's cheeks again. 'I was not raped.'

'Indeed she was not,' Lithgow said.

The man nodded. 'At least you agree on that. As for me, I don't know what happened here tonight, but——'

'No,' Arden snapped, 'you certainly do not, but I can tell you one thing for certain. This man——'

'This man,' he said with a little smile, 'is the reason you were too busy to join me this evening, *señorita*.' His gaze went to Lithgow, sliding over the pale face, the fine English wool suit, the gold Rolex winking from beneath a hand-tailored cuff. 'And I can easily see why he would be more to your liking.'

Arden flushed darkly. 'I've no idea what that's supposed to mean.'

'Haven't you?'

Arden took a deep breath. 'All right,' she said, 'all right, this is enough. I am not going to stand here, in my own bedroom, and—and defend myself against a pack of lies!'

Lithgow sank down on the edge of the bed, his shoulders slumped, the very portrait of despair. 'I'm so upset,' he whispered. 'Nothing like this has ever happened to me before. I should have known. She asked me to stop by and accompany her to the party——'

'I never did,' Arden said furiously. She spun towards the stranger. 'Dammit, do I look as if I'm going to a party?'

The green eyes narrowed and swept over her again, and even though her robe was tightly closed Arden felt as if that gaze were stripping her naked. After a moment, his eyes met hers and a muscle knotted in his cheek.

'That depends on what kind of party you mean.'

Arden sprang forward, her hand upraised, but he caught it easily, his fingers curling around her wrist, pressing down against the nerves that lay in the soft underside so that she gasped with pain.

'You have already miscalculated in your dealings with one man tonight, *señorita*. I urge you not to make the same mistake with another.'

'You,' she hissed, 'you——'

The bed creaked as Lithgow rose to his feet. He walked forward slowly, then he cleared his throat.

'*Señor*,' he said, 'have you a family? If you do, you will understand my concern for those nearest and dearest to me.'

The stranger gave a little laugh. 'Without question, *señor*.'

Arden blew out her breath. 'I don't believe this,' she said. 'Has the world gone crazy? Isn't anyone concerned about me? *I'm* the one who needs protecting; *I'm* the one who was——'

'I should never have let this—this Jezebel lure me to her room to—to try and destroy me.'

'He's lying,' Arden said angrily. 'Don't you hear it in his voice? Can't you see it in his face?'

The stranger didn't even look at her. 'If you're asking me to be discreet——'

'Yes. Exactly. As one man to another——'

'You have my word on it, *señor*.' He turned slowly towards Arden. 'Unless, of course, the *señorita* is correct, and you are lying.' Lithgow began a sputtering protest, but the stranger silenced him with a look. He turned to Arden, who gave him a hesitant smile.

'Thank you,' she said. 'I kept hoping he couldn't take you in, but I wasn't——'

'There would be no point in my pledging my silence, if that is the case,' he said softly, his eyes locked with hers, 'since the lady will wish to call the police and press charges. Isn't that right, *señorita*?'

Arden ran her tongue over her lips. 'The police?'

'Of course. If what you say of tonight's events is true, you will call them and I will tell them what I saw when I first entered the room, you and this gentleman lying in each other's arms, on that bed.'

'We weren't in each other's arms,' she said, her face white. 'I mean, we were, but only because—because he was trying to force me to—to——'

'Yes, so you've said.' He smiled, and Arden thought it was the coldest excuse for a smile she had ever seen. 'The question is, do you wish to make that same statement to the authorities?'

'Yes. Of course. I—I——'

She fell silent. She would not only be making it to the authorities, she thought frantically, she would be making it to her employers also, and who would they believe, her—or one of their own?

'Well?'

Arden looked up. The man was watching her, all attempts at pleasantry gone from his face. 'What will it be, Señorita Miller? Shall I accept your version of Rashomon, or his?'

Her gaze flew to Lithgow; she saw the faint gleam of perspiration on his brow and told herself to remember that one sign of weakness, for she suspected it would be her only victory in this ugly encounter, and then her shoulders slumped.

'Get out of my room,' she whispered. 'Both of you. Get out, do you hear me? Get out!'

Lithgow breathed a sigh of relief. 'Thank you, sir, thank you.' He stuck out his hand 'If I can ever be of assistance . . . ?'

The stranger looked at the outstretched hand as if it were diseased. 'I have no more use for men who ignore the rules of morality than I have for women who invite them to do so.' He nodded to Arden. '*Buenas noches, señorita*. It is my fond wish that our paths do not cross again.'

Tears of rage blinded her as he turned and strode from the room. 'You can count on it,' she called out as she hurried after him. 'You can absolutely——' he threw open the door, stepped into the hall, and vanished. 'Count on it,' she whispered, her voice breaking. She fell back against the wall and put her hand to her mouth just as Edgar Lithgow came marching past.

'You needn't show up at the office tomorrow, Miss Miller,' he said coldly. 'I'll have one of the other girls pack your things for you.'

'You won't get away with this,' Arden said in a trembling voice.

Lithgow smiled. 'I already have,' he said as he swept out the door.

Arden closed her eyes as the door slammed shut after him.

The worst of it was, he was right.

CHAPTER THREE

A NIGHT'S fitful sleep and the bright dawning of the Costa Rican sun combined to change Arden's perspective. Last evening's despair gave way to indignation and then to fury. She had been treated shabbily—although there had to be a better word than that to describe what Edgar Lithgow had pulled on her.

And he'd never have been able to get away with it without the help and support of that damnable drifter. It was amazing how quickly the two men had joined forces against her. Arden's mouth turned down as she zipped up the skirt of her blue gabardine suit. Apparently, you didn't have to travel in the same social circle to come to the aid and assistance of a brother rat!

But Lithgow would be on his own this morning. He wouldn't have the stranger to back him up. God, how she despised that man! She grimaced as she brushed her hair back from her face. Lithgow was bad enough, but the other man—how *dared* he take Lithgow's side, all but calling her a slut and a liar?

Rashomon, indeed, she thought as she slammed the door to her room and set off down the hall. Not all the clever literary references in the world could disguise the simple truth. The man was an arrogant bastard, a male chauvinist of the worst sort. He'd shown what he thought of women during their first encounter, when he'd tried to pick her up. What had come later—his incredibly easy switch from rescuer to accuser—had only proved it to be true.

28

And he'd probably got an extra kick out of coming to Lithgow's assistance. After all, she'd spurned his advances, hadn't she, and probably wounded that delicate male ego of his——

Arden caught her breath. The door to the stranger's room swung open just as she reached it—but it wasn't he who stepped into the hall, it was the chambermaid, dragging her cleaning cart after her.

'Good morning,' Arden said with a little smile of relief.

The girl nodded. *'Buenos dias, señorita.'*

Arden glanced into the room as she walked past it. It was empty, the bed made and ready for the next guest. He was gone then, she thought, and thank God for small favours.

She had no wish to ever lay eyes on his face again. If she did, she might well finish what she'd started last night and punch him right in the jaw.

There was a lilt to her step as she marched towards the lift. More to the point, his absence was her ace in the hole.

It meant that, today, Edgar Lithgow was strictly on his own.

Arden's counter-attack was carefully planned. She'd spent the hour before dawn plotting it from start to finish. She would get to work a little late, just late enough for Lithgow to be lulled into thinking she'd accepted his growled command that she not show up at the office again. The nerve of him! *She* had done nothing to be ashamed of, and the very first thing she intended to do was make that point—forcefully—to her former boss, for that was exactly what he'd be, as of this morning, after she'd made her short but pointed speech.

'You're right,' she'd say, after she'd marched into his office and shut the door, 'I won't press charges—as-

suming you arrange immediately for my transfer back
to the New York office and for my immediate promotion to administrative assistant.'

If he gave her one moment's argument—if he did,
she'd—she'd...

She'd what? She'd collapse like a deflated balloon,
that was what, because the only thing worse than the
prospect of letting Lithgow get away with this was the
thought of having to stand up in a courtroom and describe the humiliation of what had happened. Even worse
would be having to explain things to Lithgow's bosses.
They were all the same, his kind of people; she could
almost see the knowing little smiles of disbelief they'd
give each other.

But things would never get that far. Lithgow wouldn't
call her bluff; he wouldn't dare. Late last night, after
she'd calmed down enough to think, she'd realised that
her boss had as much reason to want to keep this quiet
as she. Hell, he might even have more! He'd ticked off
his sterling qualities for the stranger's benefit, his community and church affiliations, his status in the
company—none of them would change him from the
lowlife he was into the decent man everyone believed
him to be, but that was all the more reason he wouldn't
want a charge of sexual harassment hanging around his
neck.

'*Buenos dias, señorita.*'

Arden looked up from the menu. 'Good morning,'
she said, and then she hesitated. Was the waiter looking
at her strangely? Come to think of it, had the
chambermaid given her this same off-centre smile, as if
she knew something Arden didn't?

She gave a little laugh as she set the menu aside. That
was just what she needed now, a touch of paranoia to
top things off.

'I'll have the melon,' she said briskly in Spanish, 'and toast. And a pot of coffee, please.'

She wasn't hungry, despite having never had supper last night, but there was still time to kill and besides, she'd need all the strength she could garner for the confrontation that lay ahead. Methodically, she ate everything that had been served her, washed it all down with three cups of strong black coffee, then pushed back her chair and rose from the table.

The waiter materialised from out of nowhere and held out a small silver tray bearing the bill for her meal. Arden sank back into her seat and sighed. He wanted her to sign her name and room number, which was fine. It was just that the ritual was never the same. Sometimes you were asked to sign, and other times whatever bill you'd run up was automatically charged to the company's account.

'I'll need a pen,' she said. The waiter shrugged. '*Una pluma, por favor*, so I can sign for my breakfast.'

He gave her an embarrassed smile. 'I am sorry, *señorita*, but I cannot accommodate.'

Arden sighed. 'No problem,' she said, opening her bag and digging into it. 'I have a pen in here somewhere, if I can just——'

'I meant that I cannot permit you to charge the meal to your room.' She looked up, startled. 'It is not my decision,' he said quickly. 'It is the decision of Señor Arondo.'

There it was again, that peculiar little smile. A chill of premonition danced along Arden's spine, but she told herself she was over-reacting. Arondo was the hotel manager, but he'd only been here a couple of weeks. A screw-up was more than likely.

She dug some notes from her purse and tossed them on the tray. 'Never mind,' she said with a quick smile. 'I'll stop by later and sort things out.'

She made her way to the parking area and headed for the place where she always parked her car. But the green Ford wasn't there. The slot was empty.

Arden swung around in a circle. Had she forgotten where she'd parked it? It didn't seem likely, but anything was possible on a morning like this. The lot wasn't very big; she would be able to see the car in an instant and——

It wasn't anywhere to be seen. The chill came again, this time sending a shudder through her bones. Don't bother showing up at work, Lithgow had said, and this morning she'd had to pay for her breakfast—a breakfast that should have gone on the company tab—and now her company-supplied car was missing. It took no great stretch of the imagination to realise what had happened.

Lithgow had already eliminated her as an employee. He'd taken back all the perks of her job.

Arden's eyes narrowed. Was he really so sure of himself? Well, he was in for a big surprise.

'Get ready, Mr Lithgow,' she muttered under her breath, 'because you're not going to get away with this!'

Without a car, what should have been a few minutes' trip to work became a half-hour walk. It was a hot morning and Arden felt sweaty and dishevelled by the time she reached her office. She longed to stop in the ladies' room to splash cool water on her face, touch up her make-up and fix her hair, but the line between giving Edgar Lithgow enough time to build up a sense of false security and losing the edge she wanted was a narrow one.

It was better to confront him right away, she thought, pushing open the door to his outer office...

She stopped dead in her tracks. Julie Squires was sitting at Arden's desk. The s.o.b. had certainly moved fast, she thought grimly, and made her way quickly across the room.

'I want to see Mr Lithgow,' she said.

Julie shifted in her chair. 'I'm afraid he's not here.'

Arden's brows lifted. 'Really,' she said coldly.

'It's the truth, honest!'

Arden folded her arms. 'No problem,' she said. 'I'll wait.'

'But he won't be back for a couple of days,' Julie said, looking as if she'd rather be anywhere than here.

'Listen,' Arden said tautly, 'I've sat in that seat, remember?'

'I don't know what you——'

'I've smiled just as politely as you and lied through my teeth so I could turn away unwanted visitors for that man!'

The other girl shook her head. 'I'm telling you the truth! Mr Lithgow was called out of town on urgent business.'

'What urgent business?'

'I don't know. He didn't——'

'When will he be back?'

Julie shrugged. 'I don't——'

'I have to see him, Julie,' Arden said urgently. 'You've got to tell me where he is!'

'I swear, I don't know.' The girl looked around, then leaned forward over her desk. 'What happened?' she whispered. 'I was shocked—we all were—when Lithgow announced he'd had to fire you.'

'Is that what he said?'

'Uh huh. He left something for you. I was supposed to send it over to the hotel, along with your things, but since you're here...' Julie took an envelope from her desk. 'There's a cheque in it,' she said. Her eyes seemed to narrow just a bit and that same damned smile, the one Arden had seen on the faces of the chambermaid and the waiter, bloomed on her lips. 'It's for a lot of money. And he drew it on his own account, not the company's.'

Arden felt a flush rise in her cheeks. 'You certainly know a lot about it.'

The girl shrugged. 'He wrote the cheque while I was standing at his desk. I couldn't help but see it, could I?'

Arden ripped the envelope open without ceremony, pulled out the cheque, and stared at it. It looked as if Edgar Lithgow had decided not to count on intimidation alone to keep her silent. The cheque was for twenty-five thousand dollars.

Julie cleared her throat. 'See what I mean?'

The women's eyes met. 'Yes,' Arden said carefully, 'I do.' With slow, deliberate movements, she tore the cheque in half and went on tearing it until it had been reduced to white confetti, then let it fall like snowflakes over the desk. 'Tell Mr Lithgow he can stuff that wherever he likes,' she said, trying to keep her voice from trembling, and she turned sharply and strode from the room.

By the time she'd gone a block, she was calling herself all kinds of fool.

What had it got her, that stupid bit of drama? She had destroyed Lithgow's cheque, but damn it, to what end? She should have kept it and...

No. She could never have done that. But she could have cashed it and kept at least enough money to get her home. One of the great benefits of this job had been that her room and board were all paid for and so she'd sent most of her pay home. Her mother had been ill last year and Arden had been slowly whittling down the medical bills.

Wait a minute! Her steps slowed. The company owed her severance pay, if nothing else, and a return ticket home. She could go back and demand them...

But what was the point? Lithgow would have to approve such arrangements, and he had conveniently vanished. Well, he couldn't stay away forever. A few days, Julie had said. Arden's shoulders straightened. All right, then. She had enough money to keep going that long. The minute he returned, she'd confront him, demand that he issue a cheque for the severance pay due her and meet his other obligations to her, too, including paying her air fare back to the States.

It was the least he owed her.

The days passed, but Lithgow didn't turn up. His trip had taken him deep into new markets in South America, Julie said when Arden telephoned the office the third time late one afternoon, and he wasn't expected back for several weeks.

Arden thanked her, hung up the phone, and put her head in her hands.

Now what? She couldn't take another job, even if she could find one, not without a work permit. There was always the American Embassy, but the thought of telling her story to a bureaucrat who was probably another aristo-bastard like Lithgow was more than she could bear.

And even if he weren't of Lithgow's class, he might still give her that same damning look the stranger had. There were even nights she dreamed of the way those green eyes had narrowed with contempt at the sight of her, although why she should was beyond her to under-

stand. She certainly didn't give one fig for the man or
for what he'd thought of her...

There was a knock at the door. Arden stood up slowly
and smoothed down her skirt. She'd half expected a visit
tonight. Señor Arondo had left her a curt note earlier,
reminding her that she had not yet settled her bill for
the past week.

She steeled herself, then walked to the door and opened
it. But it wasn't the manager who stood in the corridor,
it was Alejandro, the bellboy, and he was carrying a
covered tray.

Arden breathed a sigh of relief.

'Alejandro,' she said, 'you've made an error. I didn't
order——'

'*Buenas noches, señorita*.' The boy flashed her a quick
smile. 'Your supper.'

If only it were her supper. She wasn't in the mood to
go out to eat tonight, but she'd given up ordering room
service—it was too expensive. In fact, she'd given up
eating in the hotel. The last couple of days, she'd found
it much more economical to take her meals at a little
shop around the corner.

'I'm afraid not,' Arden said. 'That's what I'm trying
to tell you, Alejandro. I didn't——'

The boy winked as he moved past her into the room.
'I hope the order is right,' he said loudly.

Arden frowned as she let the door swing shut.
'Alejandro, what's this all about?'

'I had to have an excuse to come to your room,
señorita.' He put down the tray and smiled at her.
'Otherwise, I would have got myself in trouble.'

'I don't understand.'

'I am here on my own behalf. No. That is not correct.
I am here on behalf of my cousin, Pablo.'

Arden blinked. 'Your cousin?'

'Señorita Miller, please believe me when I say I have no wish to embarrass you, but...' The boy caught his lip between his teeth. 'But we hear things,' he said, rushing the words together. 'It is said that you—ah—that you had a falling-out with Señor Lithgow and that is why you no longer work for his company.'

She blew out her breath. 'Well, that's one way to put it.'

'It is said, as well, that—that you need money. And—and——'

Her eyes focused on the boy's reddening face 'And?'

'And that is where my cousin enters the picture.'

Arden shook her head. 'I'm afraid I don't understand.'

'Well—well, Pablo knows of this difficulty of yours, *señorita*. And he would like the chance to offer you a proposition.'

Her expression hardened. 'Would he?' she said in a flat voice.

'Oh, yes, absolutely. Pablo lives an hour's drive from here, in a very big house. A mansion, you would say.' The boy's face lit. 'It is beautiful there. There is a pool to swim in, and horses to ride—oh, there are all manner of beautiful things to enjoy. And Pablo says you are the perfect woman for him.'

'Indeed.'

Alejandro was not impervious to the growing frigidity in Arden's face and voice.

'I told him that such an offer might embarrass you,' he said with obvious discomfort, 'but he was determined I speak on his behalf.'

'Yes, I can just imagine.' Arden slapped her hands on her hips. 'Well, you can just tell Pablo that I'm not interested. The damned nerve of him—and of you, Alejandro! How could you make such a proposal to me?'

The boy's face fell. '*Sí*,' he whispered miserably. 'I told him you would say this. "Pablo," I said, "the *señorita* is a secretary, she is not a——"'

'That's right,' Arden said with feeling. 'I'm a secretary, although lately everyone else seems to think I'm——'

'—she is not a nurse. "But she does not need to be a nurse," Pablo said. "Old man Romero already has one of those," he said, and it is true. What the old man needs is a companion, someone who will read to him and talk with him, someone who is a *gringa* because no *tica* has ever been able to stand up to his temper——'

'Wait a minute,' Arden said quickly. 'What are you talking about? *What* old man?'

'Never mind, *señorita*. Forgive me for having been so impertinent.'

Arden reached out and caught hold of the boy's arm as he began to turn away.

'Alejandro, please, tell me what this is all about. Is this—is your cousin——'

'Pablo,' he said helpfully.

She nodded. 'Yes, Pablo. Is he offering me a job as his companion?'

'Pablo?' he said with a giggle. 'No, certainly not. My cousin is the chauffeur to Señor Romero, *señorita*.'

'He's making the offer for Señor Romero, you mean?'

'*Sí*. The old man has many servants but only Linda to keep him company, and——'

'Linda?' Arden repeated. She was growing more baffled by the minute. Would she ever be able to sort this out?

'The stepdaughter of Señor Romero.' Alejandro made a face. 'You will not like her, I think. But El Corazon——'

'El Corazon,' Arden said numbly, as she sank down on to the edge of a chair.

'The Romero *finca*. It is the place I told you of earlier. Pablo says to tell you that you would have your own room and bath.' His voice fell to a whisper. 'You could ask to be paid many *colones*, Pablo says, because no one else will deal with the old man. He is—how do you say— difficult.'

She sat staring at the boy. A job as a paid companion, she thought, and a lump rose into her throat. A job as a servant, that was what it was, a job she'd been destined for all her life, the same as her mother and half the female population in Greenfield . . .

'*Señorita*?'

Arden swallowed hard. Alejandro was watching her with barely concealed eagerness. As far as he was concerned, he'd just offered her the opportunity of a lifetime.

Well, if it wasn't that, it was, at least, a way to earn enough money to get her home. Did you need a work permit for a job like this? She didn't know, and she wasn't going to ask. That was Señor Romero's problem, not hers.

Still, the thought of it made her flinch. How could she dance attendance on the rich, when the thought of it made her skin crawl?

How can you sit here and wait to be thrown out into the street? a voice inside her asked with cold precision.

'*Señorita*? If you are not interested——'

'But I am.' Arden took a deep breath. 'Tell your cousin I'd—I'd be happy if he could get me an interview.'

The boy grinned as he snatched up the tray. 'I will tell him to make the arrangements.'

She closed the door after him, then sank back against it. Suddenly, she thought again of the man she'd met in the lift, of the things he'd accused her of. What would he say if he knew she was going to take a job as servant to this Señor Romero?

A bitter smile touched her lips. He'd never believe it. But then again, neither did she.

CHAPTER FOUR

PABLO drove her to her interview with Felix Romero in an ancient, brilliantly polished Cadillac limousine. There would be, he warned, three separate interviews to endure, although only one would take place today.

'Señorita Linda is away, but when she returns she will insist on questioning you, too,' he said as they bounced over a dusty dirt road, 'even though the decision of your employment is not actually hers to make. Whether or not you get the job is up to Señor Romero—and to Señor Conor, of course.'

'Who?'

'Señor Conor Martinez.' Pablo looked into the rear-view mirror. 'He is—how would say?—he is the true master of El Corazon.'

'But I thought——'

'Someone had to take charge when Señor Romero's health began to fail.'

Arden sank back against the seat. 'Alejandro never mentioned any of this,' she said glumly. 'I suppose you're going to tell me this Señor Martinez is as difficult as Señor Romero.'

'Some would say he is even more so,' Pablo admitted after a pause. His eyes met Arden's in the mirror. 'Señor Conor is of the old school. He demands obedience and perfection.'

Arden could see him in her mind's eye, a tall, white-haired Spaniard, his face marked by age and discipline, until suddenly another image swept that one aside, that of a tall, handsome man with green eyes, an unsmiling

41

mouth, and the certain belief that he could never be wrong.

'You mean,' she said, her words touched with bitterness, 'he sets himself up as judge, jury, and executioner.'

The chauffeur chuckled. 'An interesting description, señorita.'

And, without question, an accurate one. Arden closed her eyes. Wonderful. Just wonderful. She was about to sign on for a job that would make her a servant, answerable to not one man but two, a pair of elderly Spanish grandees who had no idea the world was moving swiftly into the twenty-first century.

Why had she let Alejandro talk her into this? Anything would be better than——

'We are arrived, señorita.'

Arden opened her eyes and sat forward just as a pair of massive iron gates swung open to an electronic signal. The Cadillac slowed and began moving up the long driveway, and a little shudder went through her.

Alejandro had described El Corazon as magnificent; it was a word she'd heard often from her mother while she was growing up.

'I'm going to be working for the Baileys,' Evelyn would say, and then she'd sigh dramatically. 'Their house is just magnificent!'

After a while, Arden had known what 'magnificent' meant. It was a synonym for grandiose and overdone, a way of saying that a house was far too big to be a home, had cost more money than anything should, and would surely impress the life out of anyone who saw it.

But none of that described El Corazon.

She leaned forward and stared out the window. El Corazon—The Heart—had seemed a romantic name, but this house was hardly romantic. Seen from a distance, it was large and imposing, larger, probably, than any of

Greenfield's pricey mansions. A flower-banked path bisected a wide lawn that looked as if it were carpeted with dark green velvet; it led to wide white steps and a porch whose graceful colonnades drew the eye upward to the house itself with its black trim and Spanish tile roof.

Arden sank back in her seat. What was she doing here? It was too late to tell Pablo to turn the car around, she would have to go through with the first interview, but at its conclusion she would politely thank Felix Romero for his time, then ask Pablo to drive her back to the city. And then she'd swallow what little was left of her pride, go to the Embassy, and beg for help.

Anything would be better than going to work as a servant in a house like this.

Romero was waiting for her in the library. He was a wizened old man with a full mane of white hair, gnarled hands that were tightly clasped around the ivory head of a walking stick despite the fact that he was seated in a wheelchair, and an expression sour enough to make a lemon seem sweet. After a brief few questions, he fixed Arden with a rheumy stare.

'I am told that I am not an easy man to work for,' he said brusquely. 'I have a short temper, and I do not suffer fools lightly.'

Arden thought of telling him it didn't matter because she wouldn't take this job if he offered it to her, but she decided to be polite.

'So I've heard,' she said pleasantly.

'If I ask you to work for me, I will expect you to rise early, to keep abreast of world affairs so we may discuss them, and to choose your companions wisely.'

'If I were to decide to work for you, I would rise early because I have always done so, I would discuss with you whatever topics the both of us agreed were of interest, and I would choose my companions by my own standards, which I assure you are every bit as stringent as yours.'

She waited for him to respond, aware that she would never have answered with such arrogance if she hadn't already decided she didn't want this job. Felix Romero's mouth twitched. It took a moment until Arden realised it was as close to a smile as he would offer.

'It may be that you will work out,' he said.

Arden stared at him in surprise. 'Does that mean you're offering me a job?'

'Tell Pablo to go to San José and collect your things. I will give this a try.'

He would give it a try? She lifted her chin.

'Perhaps you should ask me if I will give it a try,' she said.

Romero's mouth twitched again. 'What if I suggested we both do so, Miss Miller?'

Arden hesitated. Why not? It would be just as easy to quit tomorrow as to walk off today. After a moment, she held out her hand.

'That's acceptable, *señor*.'

Romero looked at her outstretched hand, then took it into his own. His eyes met hers and he nodded.

'Done,' he said brusquely.

After a few weeks, Arden was glad she'd agreed to Romero's proposal. To her surprise, the job was working out much better than she'd dreamed it could. The old man had a sharp, analytical mind and he enjoyed exercising it; sometimes, Arden thought he deliberately played devil's advocate just to encourage discussion and philosophical argument. He had an extraordinary orchid collection and when Arden expressed an interest in it he was more than eager to teach her the names and idiosyncrasies of the various flowers.

And, perhaps most importantly, he never treated her like a servant. Her room was not in the servants' wing but in the main part of the house, and he insisted she take her meals at his table. She knew it was childish that these things should matter to her, but they did.

Still, Felix Romero wasn't an easy man to like. Despite his keen intellect, there was a coldness to Felix Romero as well as a streak of stubborn pride that kept his attitude as rigid as his spine. And he complained long and often about his stepdaughter and Conor Martinez.

'The two of them will be here soon, and you will see for yourself what sort they are,' he said stonily one morning, as he and Arden sat in the library.

'I'm sure they're very nice,' Arden said.

The old man thumped his cane on the floor. 'Do not patronise me,' he said sharply. 'I don't like it!'

Arden sighed. 'I'm only suggesting that——'

'You are wrong, I assure you. Linda cares only for herself. She never spends time here, if she can help it.'

'Perhaps it's difficult for a young girl to live in such a remote location.'

'As for Conor,' Felix said, ignoring her comment, 'his sole concern is to usurp as much of my power as he can.'

Arden put down the newspaper she'd been reading to him. 'Why do you say that?'

'You will say it, too, Miss Miller, after you have observed how he behaves.' Felix frowned. 'Of course, he claims he is merely trying to ease the burden of running this *finca* from my shoulders.'

'Isn't that possible?'

Romero laughed. 'When you reach my age, you know that anything is possible. But my nephew——'

'Your nephew?' Arden frowned. 'I thought—I assumed he was an older man.'

'He is old enough to wish to wrest El Corazon from me,' Felix said brusquely. 'He is not an altruist, Miss Miller. I assure you, once you've met him, you will agree.'

Arden pushed back her chair and got to her feet. 'Well,' she said pleasantly, 'I'm looking forward to meeting both Señor Martinez and Linda.'

The old man smiled archly. 'They won't like you.'

She stared at him in surprise. 'Why not?'

'Linda will not care for sharing the house with a woman more attractive than she could ever hope to be. As for Conor—Conor will be distrustful of anyone who might come between him and his goal.' His brows rose. 'Conor will surely dismiss you.'

Arden's spirits sagged. Was she going to lose this job after such a short time?

'And will you let him?' she asked quickly.

Felix chuckled. 'I hired you, Miss Miller. On my *finca*, my word is absolute.'

'I hope so, *señor*. Working here means a great deal to me.'

'Not to worry.' Felix leaned forward and patted her hand. 'Now, go and find out what's happened to the coffee I asked for an hour ago.'

Arden bit her lip as she stepped into the hall and closed the library door after her. That would be the final straw, she thought unhappily, if she were to lose this position because of a selfish stepdaughter and a grasping nephew...

'*Brava*,' a woman's voice said.

Arden spun around. No, she thought, it wasn't a woman, not really. It was a girl, perhaps nineteen or twenty years of age, tall and beautiful, with a look of haughty insolence in her dark eyes, and she knew without question that this had to be Felix's stepdaughter, Linda Vasquez.

'It is a brilliant strategy, *señorita*, speaking up to my stepfather as if you were his equal, then throwing yourself on his mercy and reminding him that you are merely a woman and dependent on his indulgence. No *tica* maid would ever have thought of such a thing.'

Arden flushed but forced a smile to her lips. 'I'm not a maid, *señorita*, I'm Arden Miller, the *señor's* new companion.' She held out her hand. 'And you must be Linda.'

The woman smiled, too, showing even white teeth set against tawny skin. 'I am Señorita Vasquez,' she said, ignoring Arden's outstretched hand, 'and I suggest you pack your things while Pablo prepares the car to take you back to San José.'

'Excuse me?'

'I am in charge of the hiring at El Corazon and you do not suit my needs.'

'Perhaps you'd like to discuss this with your stepfather first,' Arden said as calmly as she could. 'I think you'll find he's quite happy with me, and——'

'You are wasting my time, Miss Miller. My stepfather is not himself and everyone knows it. As for me, I want you out of here immediately.'

The woman's rudeness shattered Arden's attempted civility.

'Since you were eavesdropping,' she said coldly, 'you know what your stepfather said. He hired me. If I'm going to be fired, it will be by him.'

Linda laughed. 'How quick you are to bare your claws. I wonder, what makes you so ready to do that?'

'I told you, your stepfather——'

'Is it the money? Are you so brave and determined because you have heard the rumours, that my stepfather is rich and no longer quite as in command of his faculties as he once was?'

Arden's eyes met Linda's. 'What are you implying?'

'I have phoned here every evening since you arrived, and each time my stepfather has told me of your beauty and your charm, of your wit and intelligence.' Linda's smile faded and her eyes turned to black ice. 'If you think I will permit a scheming *gringa* to usurp my position here——'

'I have absolutely no intention of usurping——'

'You may have fooled my stepfather, but you cannot fool me, and you most assuredly will not fool Señor Martinez. He will see straight through you!'

Two crimson circles appeared in Arden's cheeks. 'Señor Martinez will see nothing!'

'That's enough!'

The voice was male and very harsh, and it brought a flash of satisfaction to Linda Vasquez's face.

'Thank you, Conor,' she said. 'I am weary of dealing with this woman myself.'

Arden spun around, words of anger on her lips, words that died before she spoke them. Her heart thumped into her throat. No, she told herself, no, it just wasn't possible.

But there he was, backlit by the sun so that he seemed to have been forged in fire, his hands on his hips, his posture intransigent, and the contempt in his voice so familiar that she knew that this encounter would not be any different than the last.

'You!' she breathed, and she stumbled back against the wall.

The drifter who'd helped Edgar Lithgow snatch away everything she'd worked so hard to attain wasn't a drifter at all.

He was Conor Martinez, the master of El Corazon.

She wanted to say something, say anything, to assert herself, but all she seemed able to do was stare at him as he walked towards her. The white duck trousers and pale blue shirt had given way to a grey wool suit, white shirt, striped silk tie, and shoes that bore the deep, dark lustre of fine leather. But there was no mistaking the hard-as-emerald glint of those eyes, the handsome face, the aggressive stride.

'What are you doing in this house?' he demanded.

'I—I...' Arden touched the tip of her tongue to her lips. 'I work here.'

'That's damned well not what I mean, and you know it.' He slammed the door after him and strode towards her, his footsteps loud as heartbeats against the tiled floor. 'I want to know how you wormed your way into my uncle's employ.'

Arden stared at him helplessly. The shock of seeing him, of learning his identity, was overwhelming. He was directly in front of her now, towering over her, or at least that was how it seemed, that same harsh look of accusation in his eyes as there'd been that horrible night in her hotel room.

What was the matter with her? She was letting it happen again, letting this awful man intimidate her. But he wasn't going to get away with it this time. No, she thought, her spine stiffening, he certainly was not!

'It must be wonderful to be you,' she said, her voice cool and calm, in contrast to the slam of her heart against her ribs. Her chin lifted so that she was looking straight into his narrowed eyes. She forced a smile to her lips.

'So few of us go through life, secure in the knowledge we're always right—you're such a fortunate man, *señor*.'

His mouth thinned. 'When I ask a question, I expect an answer.'

'And I gave you one.'

'Let's try again, Miss Miller,' he said, very softly. 'How did you insinuate yourself into this household?'

Arden glared at him. 'That's not a question, it's an accusation.'

'When Linda told me my uncle had hired a *gringa* named Arden Miller, I thought it had to be some sort of joke. "I know this woman," I said, "and she is no more a nurse than——"'

'Your uncle hired me to be his companion.'

'Why are you wasting time, Conor?' Linda said sharply. 'Just tell the woman to pack her things and get out.'

'I want some answers first,' he said, his eyes still fixed on Arden. 'And Miss Miller is not leaving until I get them.'

'I don't owe you any answers!'

'I want to know how you wormed your way into this house.'

'Oh, for God's sake!' Arden pushed past him and strode to the centre of the room. 'I didn't "worm" my way in anywhere,' she said angrily. 'I found out that Señor Romero was looking for a companion, and——'

'And you saw a golden opportunity. An old man— wealthy, lonely, ill...' A cruel smile twisted across his lips. 'Perfect for your kind of woman!'

Colour flooded Arden's cheeks. 'That's a lie!'

'I speak the truth and you know it.' His gaze swept over her with deliberate insolence, lingering on the rapid rise and fall of her breasts, then lifted to her flushed face. 'I can hardly blame my uncle for being taken in,

Miss Miller. The last time we met, it was much easier to see your—assets. But I must admit, even clothed, you are enticing.'

Linda Vasquez gasped. 'Conor?' she said, 'what are you talking about?'

'You have no right to say such things,' Arden said furiously. 'You don't know the first thing about me.'

'I know all I need to know. You're a woman who lives by her wits...' he laughed mirthlessly '...and the other qualities she possesses.'

'And you're a liar and a bully!'

Conor's brows rose. 'I'd almost forgotten how good you are,' he said. 'Your talent for turning your victim into the villain is truly remarkable.' The laughter fled his face instantly, like a chalk drawing wiped from a slate. 'But it won't save you now, Miss Miller. I've seen your act before, and I'm impervious to it. Unfortunately, Uncle Felix isn't.'

'Your concern for your uncle is touching, Señor Martinez.' Arden folded her arms across her breasts. 'Of course, if you really felt any concern for him, he wouldn't need a companion in the first place.'

'Meaning?'

'Meaning, your uncle needs someone to keep him company, to read to him and chat with him, but since neither you or Señorita Vasquez give him the time——'

'—you offered to make up for those deprivations.' Conor's lips curled in a sarcastic smile. 'Out of the kindness and generosity of your heart, no doubt.'

Arden flushed. 'I did it because I need a job, thanks to you.'

'Because if I hadn't come along to spoil your plans at the hotel, you'd have got what you wanted.'

'Because the man you so gallantly defended that night,' she said, her eyes blazing, 'fired me from my job after you'd helped him make me look like—like——'

'Of course he did. After the little trick you tried to play, he'd have been a fool not to.'

'The point is,' Arden said coldly, 'that I took this job in good faith, and your uncle is satisfied with me.'

'I'm sure he is.' She looked up sharply but there was no discernible change to his expression. He smiled politely as he tucked his hands into his trouser pockets. 'Go on, Miss Miller. You were telling us what it is you do for my uncle.'

Arden hesitated, her eyes searching his face. Was there a chance he might suddenly have decided to listen to reason? He was watching her calmly, as if he were truly interested in what she was going to say. Well, what was there to lose? she thought, and took a breath.

'I take him for walks in the garden,' she said. 'He's been explaining his orchid collection to me——'

'Really.'

Was there more in that single word than it at first seemed? No, perhaps not. He was still watching her politely, smiling almost gently.

'Yes,' she said quickly. She smiled a little, too. 'I like flowers, you see, and——'

'Is that all you do, then? Wheel Uncle's chair into the garden and listen while he describes each of his five hundred orchids in lengthy detail?'

Arden stiffened. There was something in his voice, she could hear it; he was——

'Well? I'm waiting, Miss Miller. What else do you do for my uncle?'

'I talk with him,' she said slowly, her eyes on his. 'We discuss books and films. We talk politics and——'

Conor laughed. 'Politics? You?'

Arden's cheeks flamed. 'Your uncle says I've brought the world to his door, and——'

'But you would, wouldn't you? Worldliness is one of your greatest virtues—although "virtue" is a word that doesn't quite describe your talents.'

'You bastard!'

The breath hissed between Arden's teeth as she spun towards him, her hand upraised. Conor caught it easily and forced it down to her side.

'You tried that once before, remember?'

'I remember everything about that night!' Tears of anger rose in her eyes and she twisted free of his hand. 'I should have guessed what sort of man you were the minute I laid eyes on you.'

'But you did,' he said coldly. 'You decided that I didn't have a dollar in my pocket, which meant I wasn't worth the time of day.'

'That's not what I mean and you know it! I'm talking about the way you behaved when you came to my room, about——'

'Conor, *por favor*, what is this all about?' Linda's face was pale, her dark eyes enormous as she crossed the room to his side. 'Do you and this—this woman have some sort of relationship?'

'Just the opposite, *querida*,' he said, slipping his arm around her shoulders. 'Miss Miller wanted nothing to do with me the last time we met.' His smile faded as he looked at Arden. 'I suspect she'd have treated me much more generously if she'd known who I was.'

'I know who you are now,' Arden said coldly. 'And my opinion remains the same. You're an arrogant, narrow-minded, conceited, egotistical son of a——'

'You are not in the United States now, Miss Miller,' Conor said sharply. 'I advise you to watch your tongue.'

It was probably a good idea, Arden thought, glaring back at him. It was easy to see that he was angry. No. Not angry. He was furious, although he was managing to keep that fury tightly leashed. But the fire in his eyes and the tightness of his jaw betrayed him, and somehow that control was more frightening than another man's rantings would have been.

But she would not let him see her fright. She was done letting him push her around, letting him twist her life to suit his own distorted view of who she was.

She stepped forward, her head up, a smile of disdain on her lips for him and everything he represented.

'You're damned right we're not in the States, Señor Martinez. If we were, you wouldn't dare behave this way! Women have rights in my part of the world.'

'Women such as you have never had any rights but those men choose to give them.' Conor's gaze swept over her again, his blazing eyes all but stripping the clothing from her body. 'You have five minutes to pack your things and get out. If you don't——'

'If I don't?' she said brazenly.

'The decision to call the police won't be yours this time, it will be mine. And don't, for a moment, doubt that I will do it.'

Arden laughed. 'The police! Really! What will you charge me with? Failure to be humble enough to suit the Master of El Corazon?'

'My nephew is not the master of this *finca*!' The little group swung around. The library doors had been flung open; as they watched, Felix Romero propelled his wheelchair into the hall. His cane lay at an angle across his lap. 'Not yet, at any rate!' The old man scowled as he wheeled himself forward. 'What is going on here?'

CHAPTER FIVE

CONOR stepped forward, shouldering past Arden as he made his way towards Felix. He smiled pleasantly, as if neither his voice nor anyone else's had only seconds before been raised in anger.

'Uncle Felix,' he said. 'I'm sorry we disturbed you. How are you feeling?'

The old man's white eyebrows drew together. 'You needn't bother putting on this performance for Miss Miller's sake, Conor. I've told her how things really are between us.'

Conor's smile didn't waver. 'I see your spirits are as good as ever.'

'And what a disappointment that must be, nephew. I'm sure you'd prefer to find me less capable of defying you each time you visit El Corazon.'

Conor sighed. 'You know that I come here as often as possible. If you'd agree to let me move you to my home in Caracas——'

'Yes, that's just what you want, isn't it, that I leave El Corazon so you can snatch it from me!' Felix rolled his chair forward. 'That's never going to happen, Conor, I promise you!'

'That's nonsense and you know it.'

'It is not nonsense.'

'There's no reason to argue,' Conor said softly, 'and surely not in front of a stranger.'

'If you mean Miss Miller——' Felix reached out and took Arden's hand. 'This young woman is no stranger to me. She is more like a daughter.'

Linda made a little sound of protest and Conor put his arm around her shoulders.

'How delightful,' he said, giving Arden a cold look. 'And after so short a time. Miss Miller is a very fast worker.'

'She is more concerned for my welfare than either of you have ever been,' Felix snapped. His fingers tightened on Arden's. 'Do you see what it is I must put up with, under my own roof?'

Arden looked from Felix's angry face to Conor's stony one. She, of all people, knew that it was wrong to make quick judgements, but where Conor Martinez was concerned there was little room for doubt. Each run-in with him only did more to convince her that he was an impossibly arrogant bastard who expected the world to dance to his tune.

Still, she was uncomfortable being witness to this family war, especially since both men seemed determined to draw her into it. She withdrew her hand from Felix's and smiled uncertainly.

'Perhaps I should leave you alone to talk,' she said softly.

'Talk? Talk?' Felix banged his cane against the floor. 'There is nothing to talk about, Miss Miller. Despite my nephew's best efforts, I am still in charge of this house.' He swung his chair towards Conor, who was leaning back against the door-jamb, his feet crossed at the ankle, his arms folded over his chest, looking as insolent as he had the first time Arden had laid eyes on him in San José. 'Did I hear you correctly, Conor? Did you tell this young woman to leave?'

'I did.'

Felix's face darkened. 'On whose authority?'

Conor leaned away from the wall and walked to his uncle's side. 'Uncle Felix,' he said softly, 'please listen to me.' He squatted down beside the wheelchair, took Felix's hand between his, and looked into his face. Arden's eyes narrowed as she took in the scene. If she hadn't known better, she'd have thought he really did care for the old man. 'How can I convince you that my only concern is for your welfare?'

'You have never been concerned for my welfare!'

Conor sighed. 'I know this woman has somehow convinced you she's properly qualified for this position, but——'

Arden's patience snapped. 'Stop talking about me as if I were invisible,' she said angrily. 'I didn't convince your uncle of anything! In fact, I didn't even want this job!'

'Really.' Conor rose to his feet and gave her a quick, dangerous smile. 'You mean you were kidnapped and brought here under duress.'

Arden's lip curled. 'Don't be ridiculous!'

'Miss Miller had doubts about me, as I had about her,' Felix said, wheeling his chair forward. 'But we agreed to set those doubts aside and try a temporary arrangement.'

'Yes.' Conor's eyes glinted with barely suppressed anger. 'She's quite good at temporary arrangements.'

'Conor, you are to stop this nonsense at once! Miss Miller is an excellent companion. She is not leaving.'

'She is. I'll find you someone else.'

Felix snapped his hand on the arm of his wheelchair. 'No one else will be as well suited to this position!'

'Miss Miller is suited to a great many things,' Conor said sharply, 'but playing at being your companion is not one of them.'

'That's enough!' Arden's cry of rage exploded into the room. She strode forward and stood between the two men, her eyes flashing. 'I am not a—a bundle of laundry to be argued over!' She slapped her hands on to her hips and glared at Conor. 'You've done nothing but interfere in my life since the minute I first saw you, and I'm damned tired of it! As for you, señor,' she said, swinging around to face Felix, 'as for you—I'm glad you enjoy my company, but in all this battling over whether I'm to stay or to go you've neglected to once ask me if I'd even want to stay in a house where I'm so obviously unwelcome!'

A moment of silence followed her outburst, and then Felix shot his nephew a triumphant smile.

'Such spirit,' he said admiringly. 'Where would you find me a companion her equal?'

Conor thrust his hand into his hair and brushed it back from his forehead. 'I don't know,' he growled. 'But I will, I promise you. Until then, Linda can keep you company. Isn't that right, Linda?'

Linda Vasquez swallowed drily as she looked from one man to the other. 'Of course,' she said, after a moment, 'I—uh—I'd be delighted.'

The old man snorted. 'And what will we discuss? The latest gossip from Miami? The news on the *couturier* front?' He gave a bark of laughter. 'What a wonderful idea.'

Linda smiled brightly. 'We can talk about more than that, Papa.'

Felix scowled. 'I am not your Papa. You were three when I met your mother. How could I be your Papa?'

'I only meant——'

'Tell me, my devoted stepdaughter, who is your favourite poet?'

The brunette's dark eyebrows drew together. 'I—ah—I'm not really much for——'

'Your favourite writer, then. Whom do you prefer, among contemporary authors?'

Linda swallowed. 'Well, actually, I—ah—I——'

'And what would you think of the proliferation of nuclear power plants?'

Linda turned to Conor, her face reddening. 'This is nonsense,' she said. 'Tell him to stop!'

Felix spun the wheels of his chair until he was facing Arden. 'Have you a favourite poet, Miss Miller?'

'Señor Romero, please. Thank you for defending me, but I think it's time I went upstairs and packed my things.' She gave Conor a withering look. 'Believe me, if I'd known who this man was, I'd never have bothered to——'

'Answer the question,' Felix snapped. 'Who is your favourite poet?'

Arden blew out her breath. 'Emily Dickinson,' she said impatiently. 'And now, if you'll excuse me, señor——'

Romero's mouth twitched. 'A third-rate romantic, Miss Miller, with a penchant for melancholy.'

Arden frowned. 'I don't agree. Dickinson's lines are spare but they're filled with passion.'

The old man nodded. 'And what of the use of nuclear energy, Miss Miller? Do you agree with me that it will solve the problem of the declining supply of fossil fuel?'

'Yes—but then we'll have other problems to deal with.'

'Such as?'

Linda clucked her tongue. 'Honestly,' she said, throwing out her arms, 'who cares about such nonsense? This has nothing to do with——'

'Only lily-livered fools are afraid of nuclear energy,' Felix said smugly.

Arden looked at him. 'That's ridiculous, señor. Any sensible person knows that nuclear waste is——' Her words trailed to silence and she flushed. 'Your stepdaughter is right,' she said stiffly. 'I can't see what this has to do with anything!'

'Ah, but it does!' Romero wheeled his chair to Arden's side. 'This young woman has a brain, Conor, and she's not afraid to use it. When you can find me someone who is her equal in intelligence and in determination, we'll discuss replacing her. Until then, Arden Miller stays at El Corazon.'

Conor stared at his uncle in silence, and then his gaze slipped to Arden.

'Very well,' he said coldly. 'But it will be a short stay.' He looked at Arden again, and she could see the anger once again held tautly in check in his eyes. 'Perhaps, if we are both fortunate, our paths will not cross very often while she is here.'

Felix chuckled. 'You will see her at dinner. Miss Miller dines at my table every evening.'

Conor's eyes narrowed. 'Does she, indeed?' he said, his voice soft as silk.

Arden flushed. 'It was your uncle's idea, I assure you,' she said coldly, 'not mine.'

He smiled tightly. 'And does she room in the servants' quarters?' he asked, his gaze locked on Arden's face. 'Somehow, I suspect not.'

'She is not a servant, Conor. Surely even you can see that.'

'I can see a great deal, Uncle,' Conor answered without looking in Felix's direction. 'In fact, I suspect I see more than your Miss Miller wishes.'

'You see only what you want to see,' Arden said sharply. 'Men like you always do.'

'Men like me?' Conor stabbed his hands into his trouser pockets and smiled coolly as he rocked back on his heels. 'Bums, you mean. But I was under the impression you never gave them the time of day.'

'I was referring to men whose bank accounts outweigh their morals, *señor*.'

'How very ecumenical of you,' he said, his voice like the purr of a great cat. 'You don't like men who are poor, and you don't like men who are rich.'

'I didn't say——'

'And yet you've taken a fancy to my uncle, who obviously is very wealthy.' His lips drew back from his teeth in a cold smile. 'How generous of you to make an exception in his case.'

'You're deliberately twisting my words!'

Conor moved forward slowly until they were only inches apart. 'I must be,' he said softly, so only she could hear. 'Because we both know you have an affinity for men with money. They've always provided you with a source of income, haven't they, sweetheart?'

Arden felt herself tremble with fury. How she hated this man! She wanted to slap his face, tell him what he could do with his insinuations and his lies, she wanted to turn on her heel, march out the door, and never look back.

But that was what he wanted her to do, and why should she? This job was hers—Felix had made that clear enough. Besides, if she quit it would mean another victory for Conor Martinez, another defeat for her—and she'd be damned if she'd let that happen again!

'Think what you like,' she said, just as softly. She forced a smile to her lips. 'It's Felix's opinion that counts.'

She saw his eyes darken with anger but before he could say anything she swung away from him, went to Felix, and clasped the handles of his wheelchair.

'Shall we go out and sit in the garden for a while?' she said pleasantly.

'An excellent idea, Miss Miller.'

Arden pushed the chair down the hall towards the sliding glass door that opened on to the garden. There was silence behind her, but she could feel Conor watching her. At the last moment, she turned back and looked at him. His eyes were fixed on her, a cold, green light that seemed to hold her transfixed.

A chill danced down Arden's spine. For one wild moment, she wanted to change her mind, to race to her room and pack her things...

'Well?' Felix banged his cane on the floor. 'What takes so long, Miss Miller? I want to go into my garden.'

Arden took a deep breath, turned her back on Conor, and pushed the chair out into the sunlight.

Just before seven, Arden came slowly down the stairs, her hand drifting over the polished beechwood banister. Sounds drifted from below: the clink of glasses, the light sound of a woman's laughter set against the huskier counterpoint of a male voice, and she paused on the bottom step, listening not just with her ears but with her entire body, as a doe would when making her way through a forest where danger lurked in every shadow.

I don't want to go down there!

The thought rang in her head as clearly as if she'd spoken the words aloud. Her hand tightened on the banister; she closed her eyes, took a deep breath, then let it out slowly.

She was being ridiculous! She wasn't about to step into an arena filled with lions; she was a competent, capable woman and her adversary was only one insolent, egotistical male. There was no reason to have an attack of nerves because this would not be the usual quiet evening's meal with Felix Romero.

'Remember, Miss Miller, dinner will be at eight,' Felix had said when his nurse had come to collect him. 'Tonight, we will dress formally.'

Arden smoothed down the fabric of her ankle-length black silk skirt. With it, she wore a cream-coloured silk blouse, small gold earrings, and high-heeled sandals. It was as formal an outfit as she could manage. She suspected it would not stand up to whatever creation Linda would be wearing, but that didn't bother her.

What bothered her, she thought as she made her way down the rest of the staircase and along the corridor, was that dressing this way made her feel terribly vulnerable, as if she were about to sneak into a party on the Hill when she was really supposed to be going there to pass trays of hors-d'oeuvres.

It was silly, but she'd have felt much better wearing one of her business suits, a pair of sensible pumps, and a man-tailored silk shirt. Then she'd have felt more like herself—and appropriately armoured for what she was sure was going to prove to be an unpleasant evening.

Conor was certainly not finished giving her a difficult time. Arden grimaced. The more she knew about the man, the more she disliked him. He was everything she'd suspected—and more, she thought grimly, remembering the things Felix had told her this afternoon.

'This is a good place to sit,' the old man had said when they'd reached a bank of multiflora roses in the garden. 'Come, my dear. Sit on this bench and let me tell you about my devoted family.'

Arden, who'd heard enough to last her a lifetime, had shaken her head.

'I'd rather you wouldn't,' she'd said quickly. 'It's none of my business.'

But Felix insisted. 'My nephew made it your business,' he growled. 'Now come, sit down and let an old man talk.'

He talked for what seemed hours, telling a convoluted tale of investments and land acquisitions, all of them lusted after by avaricious relatives.

'I always thought my stepdaughter the most greedy,' he said. He leaned forward and put his gnarled hand on hers, 'but my nephew——'

'Conor?'

'Yes. He is the worst. A few years ago, I fell ill. Conor stepped in and took over the running of El Corazon. Just until I was better, he said, and I, in a moment of weakness, agreed. But he has not really relinquished control from that day! He says it is for my good and for the good of El Corazon but he has always coveted this *finca* and I would not put it past him to do anything he can to get it.'

Arden's eyes widened. 'Are you saying he's trying to steal it from you, *señor*?'

The old man had shaken his head. 'Why should he steal when he has only to wait and inherit?' He had leaned closer and chuckled softly. 'At least, that is what he thinks.'

Now, standing at the foot of the steps, Arden thought what a pleasure it would be to walk into the library, smile at the man who'd accused her of being a fraud and a cheat, and tell him to his handsome face that she suspected his devotion to his uncle wasn't simply the result of familial concern.

A hand fell lightly on her shoulder. 'Good evening, Miss Miller.'

Arden looked up, startled. Conor had come up behind her as silently as a cat.

'Señor Martinez. I didn't—I thought you were in the library...'

Why was she stammering like a schoolgirl? He'd surprised her, that was all. It was disconcerting to turn around and find him standing there.

Arden's throat constricted. Why did he have to be so damned handsome? Villains ought to look like villains, not like—like movie stars. At the very least, Conor should have looked more like Edgar Lithgow, with beady eyes, mottled skin, and a patch of shiny scalp peeping from beneath a swath of thin hair. There was no reason in the world for his eyes to be that incredible shade of green, for his lashes to be so dark they'd be the envy of any woman, for his hair to be so thick and lustrous and to curl like black silk against the collar of a black dinner suit that looked as if it had been custom tailored to fit those broad shoulders, flat stomach, and long legs...

'Do I pass muster?'

Her eyes flew to his face. He was smiling in a way that sent a flood of crimson racing under her skin. Damn him, she thought, and her chin came up in defiance.

'I was wondering,' she said coldly, 'what lucky soul it was who had the joy of breaking your nose.'

He threw back his head and laughed. 'You'd like to have done that yourself, I'll bet.'

She gave him a bright, fraudulent smile. 'How ever did you guess?'

Conor chuckled. 'Well, a guy beat you to it.'

'Defending a lady's honour, no doubt.'

'We had a difference of opinion.'

'Really.' She smiled coldly. 'I didn't think that sort of thing happened very often between gentlemen.'

He smiled. 'Gentlemen don't generally work on banana boats.'

'You? On a banana boat?' Arden's brows lifted. 'Next you'll expect me to believe in the Easter bunny.'

'I did a lot of things that might surprise you, in my chequered past.'

'Ah,' she said sweetly, 'I understand. You're one of those who likes to go slumming.'

'I was one of those who liked to eat,' he said with no smile at all. 'Working banana boats may be the only job you can get when you're eighteen years old.'

'What's the matter? Did your father cut off your allowance one summer?'

Conor's mouth narrowed. 'Felix cut it off,' he said.

Arden's smile faded. 'I don't understand.'

'You don't have to.' His smile returned, although there was a tightness to it. 'I wanted to talk to you,' he said. 'I was going to come to your room, but——'

'But you knew I'd slam the door in your face if you did. Yes, that was good thinking.'

'Actually, I was running late. But when I heard you leave your room, I——'

'Actually,' she said, her voice echoing his, 'I don't know why you'd come to my room, Señor Martinez. We have absolutely nothing to say to each other.'

'That's just the point, Miss Miller. I think we do.'

'You think wrong. And now, I believe your uncle said dinner would be served at——'

'Dinner can wait.'

Arden smiled coldly. 'Ah. Spoken like the true Master of El Corazon.'

'I take it that remark is supposed to have some deep meaning?'

'Only that I think your uncle made things very clear this afternoon, *señor*. You are not in charge here. He is.'

Conor's brows crooked. 'Which, you assume, puts you at an advantage.'

'It means that I can keep my job.'

'Until I find a suitable replacement.'

She looked at him. '*If* you find a suitable replacement,' she said with a thin smile.

He laughed softly. 'You're very sure of yourself, Arden, aren't you?'

'About some things, yes.'

'There's no need to sound so defensive. Self-assurance is an admirable quality. I'm just not accustomed to finding it in a woman who looks the way you do.'

'And I'm not accustomed to being insulted!'

She turned sharply and started down the hall again, but he caught up to her when she was halfway there and clasped her shoulder.

'Dammit, will you stop playing the wounded innocent?'

'Let go of me!'

'Not until we've talked.'

'We've got nothing to say to each other, Señor Martinez. We—hey. Hey! What do you think you're doing?'

She struggled fiercely as he pushed her into the darkened drawing-room, but there was no way she could combat his strength. He slammed the door, caught both her wrists in one hand, and pressed her back against the wall.

'The first thing you're going to learn,' he said grimly, 'is that when I tell you something, I expect you to listen.'

'You're a damned bully!'

'Careful,' he said softly. 'You don't really want to get into name-calling, do you?'

'I know what you are, Conor Martinez. You're trying to take over your uncle's estate. You can't wait for him to die, you want it all now!'

Conor laughed. 'Is that what he told you?'

'I don't hear you denying it.'

'What's the problem, Arden? Does it upset you to think someone else got to Uncle Felix first?'

'The problem,' Arden said, 'is that I don't know how I'm going to be able to live under the same roof with a man like you!'

Conor laughed again, but there was a different sound to it this time.

'Don't you?'

'No.' Arden squirmed against his grasp. 'You're despicable! Let me go, damn you!'

'I will.' He shifted his weight and his body brushed lightly against hers. An electric tingle seemed to dance along her skin. 'Just as soon as we get a few things sorted out.'

'Such as?'

'While you're living in this house, you'll treat me with respect.'

'You don't deserve any.'

'And that we keep our squabbling to a minimum.'

'You might as well ask for the moon!'

Conor caught her face in his hand and held it fast. 'Listen to me, dammit,' he said gruffly. 'My uncle's health is precarious. I won't have it made worse by a little bitch like you——'

'Me? Me? I'm not the one who made a scene this afternoon, I'm not the one who——'

'You and I will do our best to be civil to each other in Felix's presence.'

'Your concern for his health is touching,' Arden said bitterly. Why didn't he let go of her? His fingers were clasping her jaw; she could feel the calloused press of them against the softness of her skin. She could feel the warmth of his body, smell his scent . . .

'It won't be easy,' he said, 'but hell, you're a talented girl, Arden. You'll manage to carry it off.'

'Listen to me, *señor*——'

'My name is Conor.'

'Don't be ridiculous. I'm not going to call you——'

'I am Conor, and you are Arden.' He moved closer, so that he was almost leaning against her. 'And we are going to be the epitome of civility whenever Felix is around.'

'I understand now,' Arden said bitterly. 'You've thought things over and it's occurred to you that it's probably unwise to treat me badly if you want to stay on your uncle's good side.'

'Don't be a fool!'

'It's true, isn't it?'

Conor shrugged. 'Think whatever you like.'

Arden gritted her teeth. 'Don't talk to me that way, dammit!'

'What way?'

'As if—as if I were a naïve child. I don't like it.'

'You're right.' Conor's hand slipped to her throat and encircled it lightly. Arden felt her pulse leap towards his palm. 'You're hardly naïve. And you're certainly not a child.'

She knew, in that instant, what he was going to do. She tried to turn away from him, but it was too late. His mouth was on hers, harsh and demanding; his hand, and the weight of him as he leaned towards her, held her fast.

Don't, she said, or perhaps she only thought it, for suddenly she felt a jolt of electricity race through her blood and explode in a wave of desire. She shuddered, murmured something incomprehensible, and her mouth opened beneath his.

'Arden,' he whispered, and at the sound of her name she moaned, her arms lifted and encircled his neck...

And it was over. His hands closed around her wrists and he stepped back. They stared at each other and, for the space of a heartbeat, his eyes were as dark and puzzled as she knew hers must be.

Arden dragged air into her lungs. 'Conor?' she said, her voice tiny and baffled.

His mouth twisted, and he wiped the back of his hand across it in a gesture of complete contempt.

'Damn you to hell,' he snarled.

He spun away, wrenched open the door, and left her standing alone in the darkness.

CHAPTER SIX

ARDEN yanked back the shower curtain, stepped into the tub, and turned the water on full blast. Closing her eyes, she turned her face up to the spray and reminded herself, for what seemed like the thousandth time since the night Conor had kissed her, that she was not going to let him force her to quit her job and leave El Corazon.

That was why he'd kissed her, she thought grimly as she worked a handful of shampoo into her hair. When ordering her to leave hadn't worked, he'd turned to the lowest kind of intimidation, the sort his kind had used throughout history to put women in their place.

Arden tilted her head back and let the water sluice the suds from her hair. Well, it wasn't going to work! The bastard had caught her off guard, which was why she hadn't slapped his face, but he'd damned well better not try it again. If he so much as touched her, she'd jam her knee into that part of his anatomy where it would do the most good. Growing up in Greenfield had taught her something, by God!

At least she hadn't had to deal with him the past week. Conor had left the house early each morning, before anyone was up, and come back late, long after dinner was finished.

That was fine with Arden, but Linda clearly missed him.

'Poor Conor,' she'd pouted last night. 'He's never here. Why must he be the one to inspect the cattle and the crops? If there is work to be done, surely you have men who can do it?'

71

Felix had glowered across the table at his step-daughter. 'Someone must supervise the men, Linda. There was a time I would have done so, but now I am trapped in this chair. If my nephew wants to pretend he is Master here, let him do his duty.'

'Yes, but when will I see him again?'

'Stop whining,' the old man had snapped, and the girl's face crumpled.

Arden sighed as she shut off the water and stepped on to the mat. She had no idea how long Conor's visit to El Corazon would last. She kept hoping that one morning she'd come downstairs and Felix would announce that his nephew was gone for good, but until that day came, the less she saw of Conor Martinez, the better—which was why she was not going to hang around the house today. Besides, today was her day off and she was going to make the most of it.

'Twenty-four hours for yourself, Miss Miller,' Felix had said crisply when he'd hired her, 'and not a minute more. I do not care where you spend your time, nor how, so long as you are here when you are supposed to be.'

'Of course,' Arden had answered politely.

She smiled a little as she toweled herself dry. What she'd really wanted to say was that she could hardly quarrel with such a rule when any fool could see she'd be spending her days off right here, at the *finca*. Where could she go, without a car? Even if she'd had one, the dirt road that had brought her here went nowhere else, unless she'd wanted to pay a visit to San José—and she had no wish to do that.

But there was nothing wrong with spending her days off at El Corazon. Arden tossed aside the towel, fluffed her fingers through her hair, and strode into the bedroom. Alejandro hadn't exaggerated the estate's attractiveness. The pool was Olympic-size and surrounded by comfortable lounging chairs, and the garden that embraced the house was magnificent, filled with spectacular orchids and frequented by tropical birds of incredible variety and splendour.

She pulled open a bureau drawer and rifled through its contents. There was a wealth of other attractions, too. The library was comfortable and stocked with all sorts of books in English as well as Spanish, and there was a music room opposite that held a piano and a compact disc player and more CDs than she'd ever seen outside of a record shop.

And if she tired of reading or listening to music or swimming laps in the pool, she could always walk the grounds of the estate or even ride them on one of El Corazon's handsome horses. Learning to ride had been one of the few benefits of growing up in a town like Greenfield. An industrious teenager could always trade an afternoon spent mucking stalls for a couple of hours on horseback.

But today, Arden thought as she took a white bathing suit from the drawer, today she was going to play it safe. She wasn't going to stay around the house, where a face to face encounter with the overbearing Señor Martinez was almost a certainty. She pulled on the suit, then walked to the mirror and peered into it, frowning as she adjusted the straps of the high cut *maillot*.

She was going to spend her day at a place that seemed to have been forgotten by everyone at El Corazon, a crystal lake with a white sand bottom that lay a ten-minute walk from the house. She had found it one afternoon, when Felix was napping under his nurse's supervision, after she'd followed an overgrown path through a dense tangle of bougainvillaea and wild rose. She'd almost turned back when the flowers seemed to become an impenetrable wall—and then the wind shifted and she'd caught a glimpse of a clearing with the sky reflected in a lake of sapphire-blue.

Arden drew her damp hair back from her face and worked it into a French braid. She'd have been sitting at that lake an hour ago, but she'd waited until she was sure breakfast was finished before going down in order to avoid Conor. Why start her day off with something unpleasant?

She glanced at the clock. It was almost nine, and by now the maid would have cleared the last of the breakfast buffet from the sun-room. A book borrowed from the library, a snack of fruit and cheese from the kitchen, and she'd be all set. It would be peaceful and quiet down by the water and, best of all, she wouldn't have to even think of Conor until dinner. All she needed now were her sunglasses—and there they were, on the table near the window...

Arden paused as she reached for the glasses. There was Linda now, making her way to the pool, wearing a bikini that was little more than three triangles of fuchsia silk held together by pink ribbon. She dropped a towel and a bottle of lotion beside a white lounger, then lay down carefully, arranging her hair so it fanned over her shoulders, lifting one leg so its symmetry would show to advantage. It was an artful performance, but for whose benefit? Surely she was alone.

No. She wasn't. Conor was there, too, coming not from the house but from the garden, wearing nothing but a pair of faded cut-off denims.

Arden's breath caught. She might have known he'd look this way, his body tautly muscled and perfect under sun-bronzed skin, his hips narrow, his legs long and powerful, giving him the easy, flowing walk of a thoroughbred stallion. And that was what he was, a thoroughbred who would use his charm to get women into his bed as readily as he'd used it to get his hands on his uncle's money.

Conor came to a dead stop. A frown creased his face; he cocked his head to the side and then, slowly, he looked up.

Arden's hand flew to her throat and she shrank back against the wall. He couldn't see her, she knew that. There were sheer curtains across the glass and the sun was reflecting on the pane. Still, he was staring at her window, and if she hadn't known better she'd have thought he was staring right into her eyes.

She took a deep breath, and then another. 'Stop being so silly,' she whispered.

Still, she waited motionless while the seconds passed until finally Conor gave his head a little shake, tucked his hands into his pockets, and continued walking towards the pool.

Arden exhaled sharply. This was ridiculous! The man was making her crazy. Well, she wasn't going to let him. People could say that Conor Martinez was the Master of El Corazon, but it was meaningless. Felix was in charge here, and...

She went very still. Conor paused beside the lounger and said something to Linda, who nodded and pointed to the bottle beside her. He smiled, took it, then squatted beside her and splashed some liquid into the palm of his hand. With long, slow strokes, he began applying it to Linda's shoulders. She smiled, then stretched as sensuously as a well-fed cat. Her hands went to her hair and plunged into it; she held the dark mass up and away from her shoulders. The action made her breasts lift towards Conor. He paused, touched his hand lightly to the girl's cheek . . .

Arden spun away from the window, snatched an oversized white T-shirt from the chair, and tugged it over her head.

Let Conor Martinez and his ladyfriend play whatever games they liked, she thought as she wrenched open the door. She certainly wasn't going to stay around and watch.

Arden sighed and rolled lazily on to her belly. The sand was warm, the sun hot, and her toes were just far enough in the water so that she was aware of the delicious contrast in temperatures. All in all, she felt relaxed and content.

'Almost decadent,' she murmured, smiling to herself as she trailed her fingertips through the soft, clean sand.

After a moment, she rolled over again, then sat up and leaned back on her hands. How beautiful it was here. She was completely alone and had been for hours, with nothing but the lake, the sky, and the jewelled iridescence of the hummingbirds to keep her company.

And she was perfectly content, even without a book to read. Sighing, she closed her eyes. The only thing she missed was lunch, or, at least, something cool to drink, but she'd decided to head straight for the lake and not to make any detours after she'd observed that touching little scene beside the pool. All she'd wanted to do was get as far from El Corazon as she could manage——

'Are you trying to roast yourself to death?'

Arden's eyes flew open. Conor was standing over her, his hands planted on his hips, his legs apart, the expression on his face stony.

'What are *you* trying to do?' she gasped, 'scare me to death?'

'You're lucky I came along,' he said brusquely. 'Another few minutes and you'd be burned to a crisp.'

She glared up at him. He was still wearing the cut-offs but he'd topped them with a shirt that hung open, revealing glimpses of his muscled chest and ridged abdomen. Her gaze fell to his navel and to the silken line of dark hair that arrowed past it until it was lost beneath the low-slung shorts.

A sudden dizziness snatched at her and tilted the horizon. Of course she was dizzy, she thought irritably. Here she sat, her head held at a crazy angle so she could carry on a conversation she didn't want to have in the first place!

'What I do is none of your business,' she snapped. She started to rise, but Conor had already dropped to his knees beside her.

'Frankly, Miss Miller,' he said between his teeth, 'I don't much give a damn if you turn yourself into a french fried potato. But you won't be any good to my uncle if you end up sick. Drop those straps.'

'What?'

'You heard me.' He dug into his shirt pocket, took out a small plastic tube, and twisted it open. 'It's probably too late to matter, but I'll put some sun block on your shoulders.'

'Don't bother. I—hey!' She gasped as he began stroking his hand over her skin. 'Hey, that's cold.'

'Only because you're practically *bien cocido.*'

'I am not well done,' she said stiffly.

'If you're not, it isn't for lack of trying. Turn around.'

Did she have a choice? Not really, not when his hand was firmly on her shoulder and the feel of it told her that he was probably right, that she was probably burning instead of tanning. Arden gritted her teeth and scooted around until her back was to him.

'This is ridiculous!'

'What's ridiculous is a *gringa* with skin the colour of cream offering herself to the sun. Turn towards me again.'

She did, her body unyielding and stiff. She watched as he squeezed more ointment into the palm of his hand, then began smoothing it over her throat. His fingers moved lightly against her flesh, dancing across her collarbones to her shoulders, then slid down her arms. A chill went through her again, and she shuddered.

'That's enough.'

'Dammit, look at your legs!'

She looked down foolishly, her gaze following his. 'What about them?'

'Lie back.'

'No. I mean——' Arden caught her breath. His hand was on her thigh, caressing her skin. No. No, he wasn't doing that at all, he was—he was simply putting a layer of sun block on her, but—but——

She sat up, slapping his hand away. 'I said, that's enough! Maybe Linda likes to be petted and stroked, but I——' Their eyes met and held for long seconds, and then Arden flushed. 'You needn't have gone to all this trouble,' she said, her voice sharp as she scrambled to her feet. 'I'm going back to the house anyway.'

'Were you watching us?' She looked down at Conor. There was an amused little smile angling across his mouth. The smile grew, and he laughed softly as he rose and stood beside her. 'You were, weren't you?'

'I was not,' Arden snapped. She brushed sand from her bottom, then turned and began marching up the beach to where she'd left her things. 'I just happened to look out my window, and——'

'Linda's a child.'

'Hah!'

'I tucked her in when she was three.'

'I don't care what you did for her then or what you do for her now.'

'Then why did it bother you to see us together?'

Arden spun around. A breeze blew her hair across her face, and she grabbed the strands and shoved them behind her ear.

'It didn't.'

'Ah.' His brows lifted. 'I should have known. Your only concern is my uncle's welfare.'

'That's right, it is. Now, if you're done intruding on my day off...' She swung away, snatched up her things, and started across the sand.

'Just a minute.'

'Goodbye, *señor*,' she called over her shoulder.

'Damn it, I told you to wait!'

'And I told you, this is—ouch!' The breath whistled from her lungs as Conor's fingers curled around her arm. 'That hurts!'

He spun her around to face him. 'Of course it does, you little fool. That's what I've been telling you. You've gone and got yourself a hell of a burn.'

Arden's smile was as warm and real as a shark's. 'Don't get too excited about it. I'll still show up at your uncle's side, bright and early tomorrow morning.'

'You're damned right you will, so long as that's what he wants.'

'As for this,' she said, raising her arm and looking at it, 'it will fade to a tan by tonight. I never burn.'

'Everyone burns down here, especially *gringas*.' Conor's mouth thinned with distaste. 'You're all convinced a vacation's not a success until you've fried to a crisp.'

'Aside from the fact that you're hardly on expert on what *gringas* think or don't think,' Arden said, 'you seem to have forgotten, *señor*, that I am not here for a holiday.

I am an employee at El Corazon.' She paused for emphasis. 'Your uncle's employee, not yours.'

His teeth glinted in a cold smile. 'That's a matter for some debate, since I am the one responsible for running this ranch.'

'So Felix told me.'

'Have you been snooping, Miss Miller?' That icy smile flashed on and off again. 'Making certain, perhaps, that the old man's assets are all you hope them to be?'

Arden wrenched her arm free. 'Your uncle told me about your arrangement.'

'You mean,' he said, almost lazily, 'he told you that I'm just biding my time, waiting for the day El Corazon is mine?' He grinned at the look of shock on Arden's face. 'What's the matter, sweetheart? Did you think I didn't know he's been complaining about me to everyone who'd listen?'

'He didn't complain, he simply told me how you've taken over things here——'

'Which distresses you no end, since that's what you'd planned on doing yourself.'

'Is that why you followed me here? To make accusations?'

'Followed you?' His brows rose. 'I didn't even know you were here until I saw you stretched out like an iguana, broiling in the sun.'

'I'll bet.'

'Do you think you're the only one who comes to this lake, Arden?' He shook his head. 'This is one of my favourite spots—I found it when I was just a kid, the first time my father sent me here to spend a couple of weeks with my uncle.' He smiled. 'Felix looked me over as if I were some species of animal he'd never seen before, said he hoped I knew how to behave in polite society, gave me the run of the place, and promptly forgot I existed.'

Arden gave him a curious glance. 'You mean, Felix had never met you before? But he's your uncle.'

'I call him that, but actually he's my great-uncle. And my father wasn't exactly a favoured nephew, especially after he married my mother.'

Don't ask him to explain, she told herself, nothing about this man is of any interest to you...

'Why?' she said, hating herself as she said it.

Conor shrugged. 'Felix saw himself as the family patriarch. I suppose it had something to do with all the money he'd amassed, ranching cattle and raising coffee—he gave orders, and everybody took them.' He began walking slowly along the sand, and Arden fell in next to him. 'Everybody but my father.' He laughed softly. 'He wasn't interested in cattle and coffee. He had dreams of being an artist.'

'An artist?'

'A painter.' Conor dug his toe into the sand and kicked at it. 'But he had no choice. My grandparents died when my father was a boy, and Felix raised him. Felix had no children, so my father was the answer to his prayers—an heir to take over the running of El Corazon.'

She waited for him to say more. When he didn't, she cleared her throat.

'And?'

'And it worked—for a while. My father went to work here on the *finca*, with Felix, travelled for him on business... That was how he met my mother, during a trip to the States, to secure a loan from some New England bankers.'

Of course. His mother had been a North American. That explained the perfect English, the green eyes.

'Molly Flynn,' he said with a little smile. 'From Boston.'

And it explained that strange first name. Arden gave him another quick glance. Yes, she could see it clearly now. The man walking slowly beside her was a fascinating blend of Costa Rican and Irish-American; he had his father's macho temperament, his mother's gift of the gab, and he'd inherited the startling good looks of both.

'What are you thinking?'

Arden flushed. 'Nothing,' she said, looking quickly towards the blue water of the lake. 'I mean, I was—I was thinking that it must have been interesting, being raised by parents from such different backgrounds.'

'My father died when I was ten. Before that, he raised me alone.'

'But what happened to your mother?'

'I've no idea.' His voice had gone flat. 'I was very small when she left one morning and didn't come back.'

'Left?' Arden came to a stop and turned towards him. 'What do you mean, she left?'

Conor stooped and picked up a handful of sand. 'I mean exactly that.' A muscle knotted in his jaw as he let the sand sift through his fingers. 'She'd thought she was marrying into the Romero dynasty. But my father, the poor fool, decided that love had given him the courage to devote his life to what he really wanted.'

'He was going to paint,' Arden said softly, her eyes on his face.

'Yes. He told that to Felix. Felix disowned him, and when my mother realised that she'd married a man who'd given up the Romero money to pursue a dream, she packed her things and went back to the States.'

'But—but surely you've seen her since. I mean, she's your mother. Mothers don't just——'

'She was never a mother, except for the nine months it took her to carry me.' He swung towards her, his eyes cold. 'She was a woman who knew what she wanted and did what she had to do to get it.'

Arden stared at him. 'I'm sorry,' she said, after a moment. Her hand lifted, went out to him. 'Conor, I——'

'It's too bad she didn't stick around,' he said in that same cold voice. 'She'd have been proud of me. I'm not at all like my old man. Hell, here I am, part of everything he turned his back on.'

Her hand fell to her side as reality returned. 'Even if you have to shoulder Felix out of the way to do it.'

Conor laughed. 'Suppose I told you I ran as far and as fast as I could from all of this when I was a kid?'

She hesitated. 'The banana boat?'

'The banana boat—and half a dozen other ways to earn just enough money to get me from one day to the next.' He smiled tightly. 'The only thing any of those jobs had in common was that you didn't need a brain to do them. All you needed were muscles.'

She could believe that. His body was hard and well-toned; the times he'd taken her in his arms, she'd felt the heated power of it...

A flush rose in her face and she turned away. 'That explains a lot,' she said. 'After you realised you couldn't get anywhere on your own, you decided to make a grab for El...'

The breath whooshed from her lungs as Conor spun her towards him. 'By the time Felix began accusing me of trying to snatch this ranch from him, I'd made a fortune half a dozen times over!'

'How? By hauling bananas?'

Conor's teeth flashed in an angry smile. 'Among other things.'

'Oh, yes, I'll just bet!' Arden twisted free of his hand. 'You're wasting your time if you think that sad story of yours would make me understand why you care more for El Corazon than you do for your uncle.'

'I told it to you so you'd understand that I know all about women like you. And I'm tired of *you* pointing a finger at *me*. You've accused me of being everything from a bum to an opportunist, you've called me a liar, you've twice attempted to slap my face—have I left anything out?'

'I only gave you what you deserved!'

The anger that had been gleaming in his eyes faded and was replaced by another kind of light.

'You almost did, the other night.'

Something in his tone sent a flush to Arden's cheeks. 'What's that supposed to mean?'

He smiled crookedly. 'We agreed to be civil to each other, but——'

'I've been trying to be civil! You're the one——'

He reached out and cupped her cheek with his hand. His fingers burned against her flesh, hotter than the heat of the sun.

'—but when I kissed you,' he said softly, his eyes on hers, 'I got the feeling we might manage more than that.'

Arden felt the leap of her pulse, but her voice was steady. 'You thought wrong.'

Conor smiled lazily. 'I don't think so. Otherwise, why would you be turning such a bright shade of crimson right now?'

'I'm not doing any such thing! I'm simply——'

'No, sweetheart, you're not "simply" anything. There's nothing simple about you at all.' His arms went around her. 'Hell, no wonder the old man's so taken with you.'

'Conor, this is nonsense. You can't just——'

'We could agree to start with civility and work up from there.'

Arden put her hands on his wrists. 'I've no intention of—— '

He bent his head and kissed her quickly, the brush of his lips against hers surprisingly gentle.

'Is that civil enough for you?' he asked softly.

Arden stared up into his eyes. They weren't emerald at all, she thought crazily, they were far deeper in colour than that, they were the shade of the jungle...

He lowered his head again, his mouth settling on hers harder than before, his lips parted so she could feel not his warmth but his heat, a heat as hot as the tropic sun blazing down from the cloudless blue sky.

A soundless whimper rose in her throat. Her mouth moved under his, her hands lifted, her palms flattened against his bare chest. He whispered something against her lips and his arms tightened around her, drawing her closer, until they were pressed tightly together. The tip of his tongue darted into her mouth and heat washed through her, rising like a flame from somewhere low in her belly, sizzling through her blood and to her breasts.

'Conor,' she said shakily, 'Conor, listen—— '

'I like the way you say my name,' he whispered.

Arden closed her eyes. She was melting against him. His mouth was at her throat; he was whispering to her in Spanish, words she only half-understood. But there was no mistaking what he wanted, what *she* wanted...

No. No! What was the matter with her? He was an egotistical bastard, the kind of man she'd always despised, and he believed her possible of the worst kind of avarice...

She gave a little sob of anger and twisted her face away from his.

'All right,' she said. Her voice was thin; she inhaled, then tried again. 'All right, Conor, enough.'

He looked down at her, his eyes still clouded with desire, and nodded his head.

'You're right,' he said thickly, 'there's no sense in this.' He shifted his weight, putting her off balance so that she had to lean against him for support. 'It's time we got down to basics.'

'I know you're determined to make me quit this job, but——'

'Job?'

'Intimidation didn't work, so now you're trying seduction. But——'

'To hell with your job!'

Arden's laughter was sharp. 'I wish to God I could echo that sentiment—but I can't, thanks to you and what you did that night at the hotel. When I think back——'

'When I think back,' he said softly, 'I know that if I'd done what I should have, none of this would have happened. You were standing outside that lift, looking as cool as a queen, and I had just returned from three weeks in the back country——'

'I know this is hard to believe, but I'm not the least bit——'

'My truck broke down half a dozen miles outside town.' His hand went to her hair and he took a strand between his fingers, rubbing it gently as if it were silk. 'That's why I looked the way I did.'

'Didn't you hear me? Dammit, Conor, I don't care!'

'Ah,' he said softly, smiling just a little, 'but you should. Just think, sweetheart, if I'd made a better first impression—— '

'The only way you could have managed that would have been if the lift had dropped through the foundations and taken you with it.'

He grinned. 'I like a woman with a temper.'

'And I don't like anything about you!'

'You don't have to. All you have to do is admit the truth: that if we hadn't started off on the wrong foot that night, you'd have gone to bed with me.'

Colour flared under her skin. 'You really are crazy!'

'One night, and we'd have got all this out of our systems.'

'You're completely insane!'

'I'm honest, which is more than you are. You're still angry that I ruined the little scam you were going to run on that guy in your room, so angry that you won't admit the truth.'

Arden punched her fist against his shoulder. 'My God, you're the most egotistical, despicable, lying son of a bitch I've ever met! When I tell Felix——'

'Tell him what? That I'm on to you?'

'Listen here, Conor——'

'That I accused you of being beautiful, and desirable, and every inch a woman?' He laughed. 'My uncle is old and ill but he's not a fool. Why do you think he hired you?'

'Because—because I can talk about things with him, and——'

'I said, he's not a fool. What man wouldn't want a woman with brains as well as beauty?' His hands slid up her throat; he cupped her face and tilted it to him. 'Even me,' he said gruffly. 'Hell, I'm no better than my uncle or that poor son of a bitch you conned into coming to your room that night.' His mouth narrowed. 'The only difference between them and me is that I know you for what you are.'

Arden moved quickly, but not quickly enough. Conor caught hold of her wrist before she could strike him, the fingers of one hand encircling it like steel.

'Don't,' he said, very softly, 'not unless you're prepared to pay the consequences.'

She stood facing him, her face white, her eyes brimming with unshed tears. Her voice trembled when she spoke.

'I hate you!' she said.

He laughed. 'What has that to do with anything?'

She stared at him while her brain worked desperately for words that would tell him, once and for all, how despicable he was but before she could think of anything, he cupped the back of her head, drew her towards him, and kissed her hard on the mouth.

'I won't buy you,' he whispered, stroking his thumb over her bottom lip. 'I'm a patient man. I'll wait until you find your way to my bed on your own.'

He gave her a last, quick kiss, then turned and began strolling down the shore as casually as if he'd done nothing more than stop to comment on the weather. Arden stood trembling, watching as his figure grew smaller and smaller, and then she cupped her hands around her lips.

'Conor!' The wind picked up her cry and carried it in a flurry of powdery sand. When he stopped and swung in her direction, she took a deep, deep breath. 'You can't afford me,' she shouted. 'Do you hear? Never, not in a million years!'

She turned on her heel and strode towards the house.

CHAPTER SEVEN

THE nerve of the man! Just who did he think he was?

Arden batted a vine out of the way as she marched up the overgrown path that led back to the gardens. The answer was obvious. He was the man who called the shots, who could talk to her any way he pleased, treat her any way he liked, because he was the master of El Corazon, no matter what Felix said.

You had to give him credit, though. She'd never met anyone who could go from a chest-beating display of male arrogance and Latin machismo to tugging on the heartstrings as deftly as Conor. All that sappy stuff about his childhood, his mother's desertion, his father's death, those little hints about his having run off in his teen years—she had no idea if any of it was true or not and frankly, she didn't much care. Lots of people had unhappy childhoods. Hers hadn't exactly been a fairy-tale, either.

The bottom line was that Conor had made the most of growing up rich. He had all the characteristics of his class with none of the responsibilities. The world was his—and that included whatever females took his fancy. Women were supposed to tumble happily into his bed with wide-eyed appreciation just for the asking—or for the seducing. Arden blew out her breath. Conor had come on to her so smoothly that she'd been in his arms before she'd realised what was happening, her traitorous body responding to his expert touch, her blood pounding...

89

A startled workman shot to his feet as she pushed aside a tangle of wild rose and strode into the garden.

'*Buenos dias*,' he said, doffing a sweat-stained cap.

She mumbled a reply as she stomped past him. Actually, she probably owed Conor a vote of thanks. What had happened minutes ago had been like being doused with a pail of iced water. She felt as if she were shaking off the last remnants of the malaise that had gripped her ever since the night Edgar Lithgow—with Conor's generous help—had turned her world upside down.

What was she doing here, at El Corazon?

Taking this job had made sense—but staying on, now that circumstances had changed, didn't. She hadn't earned enough money to buy a ticket home but she had earned enough to spend a week or two in San José. By now, Lithgow would be back at his office. She would go there and confront him, demand that he give her her severance money *and* a ticket home *and* the best damned letter of reference that had ever come out of the offices of McCann, Flint, Emerson!

She felt sorry to have to leave Felix without any notice, but there were such things as honour and respect, things the Edgar Lithgows and Conor Martinezes of this world thought were owed exclusively to them. Well, they were wrong. Dead wrong. She had rights, too, and it was time she exercised them.

She took a deep breath, then marched into the library where Felix sat reading.

He took the news of her abrupt departure well. In fact, he smiled, said he'd thought all along it was nonsense for a woman as young and pretty as she to waste time in the company of an old man.

'What is more,' he said, 'I would not have needed your services eventually.'

Arden smiled a little. 'You mean, you were going to fire me?'

'I mean that I am in my ninety-third year,' he said, 'and one grows weary.'

'Oh, but surely——'

'Please,' he said with a grimace of disdain, 'do not waste my time with platitudes, Miss Miller. I have lived a long time—and although I am not particularly religious, I believe that there is something after this life. A new beginning, as it were. Don't you agree?'

'Well...' Arden hesitated. 'It's an interesting thought, sir.'

A sly smile tugged at Felix's lips. 'Yes,' he said, 'it is, indeed. *Vaya con Dios*, Miss Miller. Pablo will drive you to San José.'

She was halfway to her room when Linda Vasquez stepped out of a doorway. The girl had traded the bikini for a skin-tight dress of crimson silk and her sultry smile for a grimace of distaste.

'In the future,' she said coldly, 'you are to use the service staircase on your day off.'

Arden smiled. 'In the future,' she said pleasantly, 'you can go straight to hell.'

It was, she thought, the best possible exit line.

Pride made her want to return to the same San José hotel in which she'd roomed when she'd worked for McCann, Flint, Emerson, but logic advised against it. The hotel was expensive and her funds were limited. There was no reason to think she'd have to stay very long, but there was no sense in squandering her money, either. She asked Pablo to recommend a hotel.

'Somewhere clean and inexpensive,' she said.

He looked at her in the mirror, his eyes filled with questions, but he asked none of them.

'Certainly, *señorita*. I can take you to such a place.'

The inn he took her to was both clean and cheap. It was also threadbare and depressing, but it would do. How long could it take to settle things with her former boss?

She went to the office unannounced, hoping the element of surprise would give her an advantage. But the only person she surprised was Julie Squires.

'Mr Lithgow's not coming in today,' Julie said, once she got over the shock of seeing Arden. She leaned forward. 'What happened to you?' she whispered. 'You just vanished into thin air!'

'Well,' Arden said politely, 'I'm back now. What time will Lithgow be in tomorrow? I'd like to see him as early as possible.'

The next morning, Lithgow sat behind his oversized desk, his face set in stern lines, ready for her.

'I've no idea what you expect to accomplish by this visit, Miss Miller. Let me assure you that——'

'You owe me,' she said gently.

He turned pale, which almost made her laugh, and she let the seconds slip by before she went on.

'You owe me, Mr Lithgow—and you'll either give me what I want, or I'll make so much trouble that you'll wish you'd never been born.'

His pallor became more pronounced. Tiny beads of sweat welled on his shiny forehead.

'You can't get away with this,' he whispered.

Arden smiled. 'I want my severance pay,' she said, ticking her demands off on her fingers, 'and a letter of reference——'

Lithgow fell back in his chair. 'What?'

'And my ticket home,' she added, enjoying every moment of his panic. Her smile faded. 'And I want them immediately.'

'Of course,' he said, his relief visible in the spots of colour that suddenly rose to his cheeks. 'Of course!'

Arden sat down in the chair opposite his desk, the one where she'd so often taken dictation. She watched as he snatched up the phone and barked out orders to Julie. It delighted her to see how easily she'd frightened him. Men like Lithgow expected to have the upper hand with women. They preyed on a woman's docility and accommodating nature—but if a woman wasn't docile, if she fought for what was rightly hers, they were lost.

She had known that once, used it when rich, spoiled young men had tried to make her life miserable back in Greenfield. But Edgar Lithgow, who'd seemed the very embodiment of morality and propriety, had caught her off guard that night in her hotel room.

Arden shifted in her seat. She'd been caught off guard by Conor, as well, the times he'd taken her in his arms, the times she'd responded to his kisses. The memory was humiliating. Why had she let him make such a fool of her?

'I've made all the arrangements, Miss Miller.' She looked up. Lithgow was smiling brightly. 'You wanted a letter of reference, an airline ticket, and your severance pay.'

'Yes. All the things you surely meant to give me before you went off on your trip a few weeks ago, Mr Lithgow, isn't that right?'

He blinked. 'I assure you, I thought everything was taken care of before I left, but——' He spread his hands. 'A regrettable error.'

'Well,' Arden said briskly, 'let's make sure there are no errors this time.'

Lithgow nodded. 'Miss Squires is arranging for your ticket now, and you'll have the letter of reference within half an hour. The cheque will take a bit longer. New

York will have to OK it,' he added quickly, when Arden frowned. 'Today's a holiday back home, had you forgotten? It may take until Thursday.'

He was right, but it wasn't the end of the world; it meant only that another few days would pass before she could leave Costa Rica. Still, her stomach knotted at the thought. She wanted to leave, to go back to all the things that were familiar and safe.

'I'll have Miss Squires call you as soon as I get the OK.'

But the days dragged by, with Julie offering excuses for the delays until finally, one afternoon, Arden decided she'd had enough. She called Lithgow's office and demanded to speak to him.

'Tell him he's got a choice,' she said. 'Either he talks to me now or he talks to my attorney later.'

Lithgow came on the line almost immediately. His tone was apologetic and conciliatory.

'Miss Miller,' he said, 'I know you've been patient——'

'More than patient,' Arden snapped. 'And you've repaid my patience by wasting my time.'

'No. I have not. New York hasn't OKed your cheque, and——' He swallowed audibly. 'Please don't do anything precipitate.'

'Precipitate?' Arden laughed. 'Waiting all these days for the money you owe me is hardly "precipitate"!'

'I know—and I'm going to take care of things at once. I'll have it delivered to you within the hour.'

The phone went dead. Well, then, that was settled. All it had taken was a bit of muscle. Arden sighed deeply. She ached to leave this country, to put everything that had happened behind her. She sank down on the edge of the bed and put her head in her hands. She wanted to stop thinking about Conor, about all the times he'd made her look like a fool.

There was a knock at the door. Arden sprang to her feet and breathed a sigh of relief. Lithgow must have sent her cheque by special messenger. Smiling, she flew to the door and flung it open.

Conor! It was Conor who stood in the doorway, not a uniformed messenger.

'Hello, Arden.'

She stared at him, stunned. Her throat worked and finally she managed to whisper his name.

'Conor?' She swallowed. 'What—what——'

'We have things to discuss, Arden. And I really think we should discuss them in private.'

In private. In this tiny room, with a bed that took up half the floorspace? Her gaze flickered over him, taking in the handsome face, the broad shoulders that seemed to push against the confines of his dark blue T-shirt, then dropped to the faded jeans that hugged his hips...

'What's the problem, Arden? Are you concerned about the impropriety of having a man in your room?'

Her mouth hardened. 'What are you doing here?' she said coldly.

'I told you, we need to talk.'

'How did you find...?' She puffed out her breath. 'Of course. Pablo told you.'

'Yes.' His gaze slipped past her. 'It's hardly the sort of place you're accustomed to, is it?'

There was an edge to his words that made her flush. 'I won't be here long.'

'No.' His lips pulled back from his teeth, and he made a sound that was not quite a laugh. 'No, I'm sure you won't.'

Her flush deepened. 'Either tell me why you came here, or leave.'

Conor shouldered his way past her. 'This won't take long. I've had a rough week, so let's get this over with.'

Yes, Arden thought as the door swung shut, he must have had a difficult week. There were shadows under his eyes and lines of exhaustion etched alongside his mouth.

'Get what over with?' she asked slowly.

He didn't answer. Instead, he walked to the centre of the room and looked around. She knew he was taking in the shabby surroundings, the suitcase left on a chair and never unpacked because there was no closet, the window that looked out on a narrow alley.

'What a comedown for you, sweetheart,' he said softly.

Arden stiffened. 'Is that why you came? To insult me?'

He swung towards her, his eyes a dangerous shade of green. 'Felix is dead.'

She stared at him. 'What?'

'It happened three days ago, in his sleep.'

Arden swallowed. 'Conor, I'm so sorry. I——'

'Yeah.' The muscle in his cheek knotted and un-knotted. 'I'll bet.'

She took a handkerchief from her pocket and dabbed at her eyes. 'He said he was tired. We—we talked about it before I left the ranch...'

'Did you,' Conor said, his voice flat. 'What else did you talk about, Arden?'

'I don't know—I don't remember.'

Conor put his hands on his hips. 'Try.'

She looked at him. There was such anger in his eyes. No, it was more than anger. It was—it was rage.

'Did he talk about a new beginning?'

Arden frowned and tried to remember. 'Yes. Something like that.'

He strode to where she stood and clasped her shoulders roughly. 'And what did you say to that?'

'I said—I said, I hoped he was right, that I believed in new beginnings, too, and he——'

'You bitch!' Conor's fingers dug into her flesh as he shook her. 'I'm just surprised you left the change in his will to chance, that you didn't go round up Inez and Thomas that very minute instead of trusting Felix to do it on his own.'

'Damn you, let me go!' Arden wrenched free and glared at him. 'What do the cook and the gardener have to do with this? What are you accusing me of?'

'They witnessed the hand-written codicil Felix drafted to his will an hour after you left El Corazon.'

'What's that got to do with me?'

Conor laughed unpleasantly. 'Ah. Now she's going to try and play dumb!'

'Listen, Conor, either get to the point or get out!'

'The codicil is short and sweet. "To Arden Miller," Felix wrote, "I leave my beloved *finca*, so that we may all have a new beginning."'

Arden reached out and clasped the back of the chair. 'I don't believe you!'

Conor's smile was terrible in its coldness. 'He left you El Corazon. The whole thing, sweetheart. The house. The land. The crops and the cattle. All of it, right down to the pots in the kitchen.'

Her throat worked. 'No,' she whispered, 'he couldn't have.'

'You mean, he shouldn't have. But he did. And if you think, for one minute, I'm going to permit you to——'

'I'm not,' she said in a rush, 'I mean, I don't expect——'

'Everything I thought about you is true, isn't it? You wormed your way into the confidence of an old man and——'

'Stop it, Conor! You don't know what you're saying. I'm trying to tell you, I never——'

'You won't get El Corazon, not while I'm here to stop you.'

Arden's eyes flashed. 'For the last time,' she said, 'listen to me before you make a complete fool of yourself. I never asked Felix for anything. And I won't accept——' There was a rap at the door. She uttered a sharp oath, swung around and threw it open. 'What is it?' she snapped.

A boy stood in the dimly lit corridor, a large envelope clutched in his outstretched hand.

'I am sorry to disturb you, *señorita*, but Señor Lithgow said to deliver this to you at once.'

Arden snatched the envelope from him and tore it open. Her hand stilled. These were the documents she'd waited so long for. Minutes ago, they'd meant everything. Now, they were nothing but an intrusion.

She closed the door, leaned her forehead against it, and took a deep breath. Well, Lithgow had finally come through. Tomorrow morning, she'd put a few thousand miles between herself and Conor Martinez, and it wouldn't be a moment too soon. As for the news he'd just brought her—Arden closed her eyes. She didn't want El Corazon. God, no!

Of course, Conor would never believe her, no matter how many times she tried to tell him. Well, there had to be a way to legally renounce an inheritance. That was the first thing she'd do when she got home, find herself a lawyer and have him draw up the papers to——

'Lord, what a cold-hearted bitch you are!'

Arden's hands balled into fists. Be calm, she told herself, don't answer him back, no matter what awful things he says. Just tell him to leave, and after he does——

'I've known a lot of women in my time, but never one as ruthless or as greedy as you!'

She swung around, determined to say nothing, to defend nothing, simply to point to the door and order him out...

Conor was holding an envelope out to her. 'You dropped this,' he snarled.

She stared at the envelope as he shoved it into her hand. The blood drained from her face. It had Edgar Lithgow's name on it—and it was stuffed with American banknotes.

'Conor.' Her eyes flashed to his. 'I can imagine what you're thinking. But you're wrong.'

'No.' He laughed, and Arden thought she'd never heard a sound like it before. 'No, sweetheart, I was never wrong, not about you.' He caught hold of her wrist and drew her forward, until they stood only inches apart. 'I just wish to hell I hadn't been so gentle with you the last time we met.' His lip curled. 'But then, women like you never get what they deserve.'

Arden felt herself go cold as stone. She stared at him in silence while she fought for control, and then she forced a smile to her lips.

'You're wrong,' she said. 'Women like me get exactly what they deserve. That's why I'm going to take everything your uncle gave me.'

She wrenched her arm from his grasp and turned her back to him, furiously blinking back the tears of frustration and despair that threatened to spill from her eyes. Quickly, she slammed her suitcase shut and dragged it from the chair.

'Where are you going?' Conor demanded as she reached for the doorknob.

'To the *finca*.' Her voice trembled this time, and she counted silently to ten before she continued. 'El Corazon is mine now.'

'You're ahead of yourself, lady. Felix's will hasn't gone through probate yet.'

'What would you suggest, then? Shall we find a judge and ask him if he thinks Felix Romero would really want his heir to rot in a dingy hotel room while the nephew he despised takes up residence in the house he left to her?' She looked back at him, her smile glittering like ice. 'I'll bet the press would jump on the story with both feet.'

Conor's face whitened. 'El Corazon is mine,' he said harshly. 'If you think I'm going to let you spend so much as ten minutes there without me to watch you——'

'It's a big house,' Arden said. 'And I'm a generous woman. You can stay in your old room, Conor—just so long as you keep out of my way.'

She marched from the room with Conor hard on her heels.

The suitcase was heavy but blind anger kept her from feeling its weight until she was halfway down the narrow staircase that led to the lobby. But by the time she reached the front desk, she felt as if she were carrying a load of bricks. Her fingers hurt, her wrist burned, and her arm felt as if it were being dragged from its socket.

And Conor knew it. She could hear his footsteps behind her, hear him whistling tunelessly as she dragged the bag across the floor, but he hadn't made any offer of assistance.

Well, she thought grimly, that was just fine. She didn't want anything from him, didn't need anything from him—it was bad enough they were going to have to ride back to El Corazon together, but what choice did she have except to climb into the vintage Cadillac alongside

Conor? Not that she'd have to look at him, once they were inside the car. The limousine was as big as a boat; she could sit in one corner and Conor in the other, and if and when she felt the need to ask a question, she could ask it of Pablo.

The manager peered over the reservation desk, looked at Arden as she lugged the case in his direction, then looked at Conor, still strolling calmly behind her, and his brows rose into his hairline.

'*Buenas tardes, señorita*.'

Arden nodded. 'Good afternoon,' she panted. With a little groan, she dropped the suitcase to the floor and stepped up to the desk. 'I'm checking out,' she said. 'Here's my key.'

'Certainly.' He took the key from her and cleared his throat. 'Do you—ah—do you need any assistance, *señorita*?'

What she needed, Arden thought, was someone to march over to Conor Martinez and punch him in the jaw.

'If you give me a moment, I'll get the boy to help you.'

'She's managing just fine,' Conor said pleasantly.

Arden spun towards him. He was lounging against a chair, examining his finger nails.

'*Señorita*? Shall I call the boy?'

Conor looked up and their eyes met. 'On second thought,' he said with a tight smile, 'perhaps you should. I suspect the *señorita's* going to need all the help she can get.'

The words, Arden knew, had a double meaning. It was a ridiculous challenge—and yet, she found herself rising to meet it.

'Thank you, *señor*,' she said, her eyes still fastened to Conor's, 'but it isn't necessary. I can manage very well on my own.'

She took a breath, grasped the handle of the suitcase, hoisted it up and marched to the front door. It took enormous effort to shove the door open, more effort still to wrestle the luggage out to the pavement, but she managed. She managed, as well, to let the door slam in Conor's face. It was the one thing that had happened in the past hour that made her smile.

With a gusty sigh, she dropped the bag to the ground and wiped the back of her hand across her forehead. The Cadillac wasn't out front, as she'd expected, but then, this part of the city was fairly crowded with commercial establishments and small shops which made traffic fairly heavy. Pablo had probably had to drive off and circle the block while he waited for Conor to reappear. Arden's mouth turned down. That was what the rich made their chauffeurs do all the time; she'd seen it happen often enough along Greenfield's trendy main street back home.

An expensive car would pull to the kerb, a chauffeur would leap out, open the rear door, and a figure would emerge.

'I'll be back in an hour,' he or she would say with a dismissive wave, and the chauffeur would drive off, return dutifully at the appointed time—and then have to circle the block endlessly, waiting for his thoughtless employer to reappear.

Arden lifted the scooped neckline of her dress away from her skin and fanned it lightly back and forth. It was quite warm, far warmer than usual in this city comfortably situated on a mountain plateau. The Cadillac, at least, had air-conditioning. Pablo had offered to turn it on last time he'd taken her to the *finca* but she'd turned him down, preferring the sweet scents of wildflowers to the smell of artificially chilled air, but this time she'd let him turn it on full blast. In fact, she thought grimly, giving Conor a glance out of the corner of her eye, she'd *tell* him to turn it on the instant she climbed into the car. She might as well establish who was in charge, right from the beginning...

From the beginning. What had Felix said about beginnings? Something about—about——

'Have you got your second wind yet?'

She looked up. Conor was looking at her, smiling politely, speaking in that same pleasant, unemotional tone he'd used when he'd spoken to the desk clerk.

Arden's brows arched. 'Are you speaking to me?'

'I must be,' he said, still pleasantly. 'I don't see anybody else here, do you?'

'Well, then, thank you very much for your interest in my health. But I assure you——'

'Is that a yes?'

Her eyes narrowed. 'It's more of a "none of your business",' she said coldly.

He nodded. 'I see. In that case, I won't bother about whether or not you can keep up with me, I'll just set a pace and let *you* worry about meeting it.' He stepped away from the building and set off down the street. His gait was not quick but it was steady; in a few seconds, he was several yards away.

'Hey.' Arden got to her feet. 'Hey—where are you going?'

Conor turned and looked at her. 'To the car.'

She stared at him. 'Isn't Pablo going to pick us up?'

A smile curved across his mouth. 'Sure—if you want to wait until he returns from visiting his mother on the coast.'

With that, he turned and began walking. She stared at his retreating figure and then she groaned softly, grabbed her suitcase, and staggered after him.

She kept him in sight for the next few minutes, but after a bit it was impossible to manage. It was easier to walk with her head down, concentrating her energy on putting one foot in front of the other. Left, right, left, right, left——'

'You damned little fool!'

She looked up, startled, as Conor seemed to materialise out of the air. He snatched the suitcase from her, grasped her by the elbow, and hustled her along beside him.

'You'll do anything to infuriate me, won't you?'

'Infuriate you?' Arden gaped at him as she struggled to match his increasingly swift pace. 'Are you crazy? What does me carrying my suitcase have to do with you?'

'Everything,' he snarled.

'I don't see how——'

'Don't you?'

'No. No, I——'

'You're on your way to El Corazon, not at my invitation but because you somehow convinced my uncle to will it to you.'

'I did nothing of the sort! And I resent you saying——'

'I don't want you there. I don't even want you on the same planet as I am!'

Arden smiled sweetly. 'Is Linda as eager for my company as you are?'

'Linda took her grief to Miami after the funeral,' Conor said, his words laced with sarcasm.

'You mean, you and I will be alone?' she said, her smile fading.

Conor shot her a furious glare. 'It's one hell of a romantic thought, isn't it? You and I, your miserable luggage, driving off into the sunset in my car——'

'You mean, *my* car,' she said coldly.

He looked at her again. 'What?'

'The Cadillac belongs to El Corazon. That makes it mine.' She tried to wrench her arm free of his grasp, but it was impossible. 'And I did not ask you to carry my suitcase. I didn't ask you to do anything! I wouldn't, not if you—what are you doing?' she demanded as he all but threw her against the side of a dusty, disreputable looking vehicle.

'Unlocking the door to my Bronco,' he said through his teeth, 'preparatory to tossing either you or your luggage into the back seat—depending on whether or not I can get control of my temper in the next five seconds.'

Arden stared foolishly at the car. 'But—this isn't the Cadillac,' she said.

'A brilliant deduction.'

'It's an old Jeep!'

'It's a Bronco.'

'I don't care if it's a rowboat! I'm not getting into that thing with you.'

'Ah, my apologies, *señorita*.' Conor made a sweeping, dramatic bow. 'I know my humble vehicle's not up to your standards.'

No, it certainly wasn't. The Cadillac had offered the protection of wide seats and space, but this thing—this Bronco—would put her cheek by jowl next to Conor; she could just imagine how it would racket around the curving dirt road that led the last few miles to the *finca*, how she would be forced to lean in against him as they drove...

He threw open the passenger door. 'I know it's going to be a hell of a disappointment, making your grand entrance in this instead of in the Caddy but believe me, no one at the ranch will care.' He smiled slyly. 'Of course, if you prefer, you could always walk.'

Arden scrambled into the car. Conor nodded, tossed the suitcase into the back, and slammed the door after her.

'Good thinking,' he said as he slipped behind the steering-wheel and stabbed the key into the ignition. 'After all, if I got to the house before you did, I might just steal the silverware.'

Arden snapped her seatbelt closed, folded her hands in her lap, and stared straight ahead.

'My thoughts precisely,' she said.

With a roar and a belch of plumy exhaust, the Bronco shot away from the kerb.

CHAPTER EIGHT

THEY reached the *finca* just after sundown. Arden was certain that Conor had deliberately aimed for every pothole and bump on the road, and when they finally bounced to a halt in the curving driveway she couldn't wait to climb out of the car.

But she didn't. Instead, she stared at the house as it rose silhouetted against the night sky, and her breath caught.

What am I doing here? she thought with a little shudder. Felix had left El Corazon to her, but——

Conor flung open his door and stepped out. 'Where do you want your luggage?'

She looked blindly in his direction. At the airport, she thought, on a plane bound for New York.

'In the same room you used before?'

No matter what had gone wrong in this family, wasn't Conor better entitled to inherit this house than a stranger?

'If you're waiting for a welcoming committee, you're in for a disappointment.' Conor pulled her door open. 'Look at the bright side, Arden. At least, the *alquacil* isn't here to arrest you.'

She blinked her eyes. 'What?'

'I said, at least the sheriff isn't——'

'I know what the word means, Conor! What I'm trying to figure out is what you meant by that remark.'

'I meant just what I said. You're lucky you're not being run in for fraud.'

'Fraud!'

'Or whatever it is you call convincing an old man to sign his property over to a con artist.'

Arden gritted her teeth. No wonder Felix had left the house to her. The only thing worse than leaving El Corazon to a stranger would have been leaving it to a man like Conor Martinez!

She threw open her door and stepped to the ground.

'My old room will do fine,' she said coldly. She started towards the house. Behind her, Conor grunted as he hoisted her suitcase from the back of the Bronco and followed after her. 'As for meals——'

'I can't hear you.'

She turned at the top of the steps and waited until he'd climbed to the porch beside her.

'I said, we'll arrange mealtimes so that we don't intrude on each other.'

Conor's eyes turned flat. 'Will we, indeed?' he said, carefully setting down the suitcase.

'I'll have my breakfast at seven, lunch at noon, and dinner at six. You'll eat an hour later. That way——'

She gasped as his arm shot past her, his hand slapping flat against the closed door.

'You're in no position to give orders,' he said sharply.

'I wasn't giving orders, I was only suggesting a workable arrangement. Surely you've no more desire to bump into me than I have to bump into you!'

'If there's any scheduling to be done, I'll be the one who does it. El Corazon is still mine—or had you forgotten?'

Her chin lifted in defiance. 'According to Felix's will—— '

'According to his will, the ranch belongs to me. It's only the codicil that says he left it to you.'

Arden smiled. '*Only* the codicil? Unless my memory's slipping, a codicil is a legally binding addendum to a will, which means——'

'Not if the person who writes it doesn't know what he's doing.'

'Come on, Conor, you can do better than that! Are you going to suggest Felix was senile? Everybody knows he was as sharp as a tack. Or that I brainwashed him into leaving me El Corazon?' She made a face. 'Don't be ridiculous.'

'Whatever you did, it worked.'

'Hasn't it occurred to you that Felix might have left me El Corazon because he liked me?'

Conor laughed softly. 'I'll just bet he did.'

Her eyes flashed. 'That's disgusting. He was an old man——'

He shifted his weight lazily so that all at once he was as close to her as a whisper.

'Right. But a man's never too old to appreciate a woman like you.'

'You know something, Conor? The more you insult me——'

'Is that what I'm doing?' He lifted his other hand and flattened it against the door so that she was trapped between his outstretched arms. 'Hell, I thought I was paying you a compliment.'

'And I don't appreciate your sarcasm!'

'It's not sarcasm, sweetheart.'

'Dammit, don't call me that!'

He lifted his hand and stroked his knuckles lightly along her cheek. 'There's not a man in his right mind could resist you.' He smiled lazily. 'Hell, only a saint or a fool would turn you away.'

'Conor——'

'Not even me,' he whispered. 'You got old Edgar to come around, and Uncle Felix. For all you know, I might tumble just as easily, sign El Corazon over to you, save you months of legal battling.'

Months? *Months*? Surely this was just more intimidation. He couldn't mean 'months'.

Arden swallowed hard. 'El Corazon's mine already.'

Conor laughed and blew a curl back from her temple. 'Maybe.'

'There's no "maybe" about it.'

He shrugged lazily. 'I'm just suggesting there are possibilities you haven't considered yet.'

Her heart skipped a beat. 'What do you mean?'

'Legal wheels grind slowly, *querida mia*.' His thumb slipped over her lower lip. 'In Costa Rica as well as in the States.' He bent his head and nuzzled the hair back from her ear. 'I know a lot of ways we could make the time pass quickly.'

His breath was warm against her skin. A tremor went through her, and she put her hands against his chest. 'Stop it.'

'Is that what you really want me to do?' he said, very softly. The night suddenly seemed very still. Darkness was wrapped around them, enclosing them in a silky universe all their own. Conor's smile faded as their eyes met. His gaze drifted to her lips and lingered there for the space of a heartbeat. '*Me encantan tu boca*,' he murmured.

I love your mouth, he'd said. The words were simple and not terribly original. Why, then, did she feel so breathless? Why was she suddenly aware of the feel of his arms around her, the quick, accelerated beat of his heart beneath her hands?

'You're beautiful, *querida*,' he said huskily. 'Very beautiful.'

He bent his head and brushed his mouth over hers. The touch of his lips was as soft as the night, but she felt its heat burn through her flesh. With the fear and desperation of a rabbit escaping a fox, she wrenched free of his embrace and searched for the right words to wound him.

'What are you trying to do, Conor? Seduce me—or swindle me out of my rightful claim to this ranch?'

But she hadn't wounded him. He only laughed softly and tilted her chin up with his finger.

'That depends on how well you perform once you're in my bed.'

Arden stiffened. 'You don't listen very well. I told you, the more you insult me, the more determined I'm going to be.'

'You can be as determined as you like.' He'd stopped smiling, and the easy playfulness was gone from his voice. His eyes, and his words, were hard. 'But you're never going to get this ranch.'

'Has it ever occurred to you that I might not want it?'

'Of course it has,' he said. 'Just as it's also occurred to me that the moon might really be made of green cheese.'

Arden reached down and grabbed hold of her suitcase. 'It would be nice if it were,' she said, 'because then a rat like you could look at the sky each night and know you had as much chance of biting into that cheese as you have of getting this ranch!'

Turning away, she pounded her fist against the door until a servant came flying down the hall to open it and then she stalked inside to the stairs and carried her bag the entire flight, down the hall, and into her room. Once safely inside, she slammed the door and dropped the suitcase to the floor.

She didn't want El Corazon, by God!

But she was damned if she was going to let Conor Martinez steal it from her!

She slept soundly but not well. At dawn, when the crowing of a rooster somewhere on the *finca* awakened her, she felt bleary-eyed and almost achy with fatigue. She lay still, fighting against the sudden desire to repack her things and flee. Why should she run? she asked herself sternly. She had an absolute right to be here. It was Conor who was the intruder, not she, Conor who ought properly to move out...

...Conor, who never ceased to confuse her. Arden shook her head as she pushed aside the blanket. He had a strange ability to jumble her thought processes whenever he was around.

No, she thought as she dressed in jeans and a cotton T-shirt, that wasn't quite accurate. He didn't confuse her so much as he made her feel unsettled, as if his very presence somehow tilted the horizon just enough to make her usually familiar world become out of kilter.

Well, she wasn't going to have any such problem today, she thought as she buckled on a small waist pack. With luck, she'd never even set eyes on him until tonight. It was just past six-thirty, surely far too early for him to be up and about. There was plenty of time to make a stop in the kitchen to pick up something light for lunch as well as to get a cup of the dark, rich coffee Inez would have just finished brewing without having to worry about running into Conor.

Arden smiled grimly. By the time he began his day, she'd be miles away.

Inez greeted her with a broad smile. '*Buenos dias,*' she said, then added, in rapid Spanish, that she was delighted to see that the *señorita* had returned to El Corazon.

Well, Arden thought with a little smile, at least someone was pleased to have her here. She drank half a cup of coffee, then tucked some fruit and biscuits into her waist pack. At the last minute, she stopped and scooped a handful of sugar cubes from the bowl on the table.

The morning was soft and perfect, as were all the mornings she'd spent at El Corazon. She paused outside the door and took a deep breath of the clean, sweet air. It was good to be back here, she thought with surprise, despite the less than pleasant circumstances. She sighed as she began plodding through the dew-wet grass. Felix had been ready for his new beginning, but was she? If only Conor...

Arden frowned. If only Conor what? She didn't give a damn what he thought. It didn't matter if he wanted her here or not. The *finca* was hers now, all of it, from the house to the rolling pastures that stretched all the way to the darkly smudged hills that defined the horizon.

A horse whinnied softly in the paddock. Arden looked to where a mare and foal stood close together, their manes tossing gently in the light morning breeze.

'Good morning,' she said as she walked towards them. The mare pricked her ears, then trotted forward and delicately accepted the sugar cube Arden held out on her palm. Arden smiled and stroked the velvety muzzle. 'Will you remember me the next time we see each other?' she whispered. She laughed when the mare snorted and bobbed her head. 'Good girl!' Humming softly, she swung away from the fence and set off for the stables.

Today, she was going to see the ranch Felix had left her from one end to the other, and she was going to do it on horseback. It would give her answers to some of the questions she had about the *finca*, questions she'd sooner die than ask of Conor. And it would keep her away from the house—and from Conor. As for tomorrow, well, she'd worry about tomorrow when she got to it.

The stable door creaked softly when she pulled it open. The sweet smell of hay and horse filled her nostrils as the door thunked shut after her.

It was darker here; shadows dappled the aisle that stretched between rows of box stalls. Arden blinked, waited until her eyes adjusted to the change in light, then began to walk slowly down the aisle. Horses nickered softly from the stalls as she passed them and she paused often to pet a silken muzzle and distribute her sugar cubes.

The sound of the door swinging open, then slamming shut, shattered the silence. She whirled around, her hand to her heart.

'Come to do an inventory of the livestock?'

Conor's voice was gruff, his posture challenging. Everything about him looked challenging, Arden thought, and her heart tumbled with a strange double beat. He was dressed as she was, in a T-shirt and jeans, but the shirt moulded itself to his muscular shoulders and chest and the jeans were so old and faded that they delineated his maleness.

'Or are you just here to do a general inventory?'

Colour flamed in her face. Her eyes swept up to his and she gave him a cold look.

'I don't appreciate having you checking up on me, Conor.'

He smiled coolly. 'Is that any way to thank me, Arden?'

'Thank you?' She put her hands on her hips. 'For what? For following me like a shadow?'

'I was on the far side of the stables, grooming Diablo——'

'Diablo.' Arden smiled sweetly. 'Of course. What else would Señor Martinez name his horse except Diablo?'

'I was grooming him,' Conor said pleasantly, 'and I looked up and there you were, trying to bribe one of our best mares with sugar.'

'Don't be ridiculous! I was simply——'

'And I thought, Isn't that charming, the *señorita's* going to the stable to count noses? Why don't I go and help her?'

Arden tossed her head. 'It's nothing like that.'

'You should have asked me for a list of our stock, Arden. I'd have been happy to oblige.'

She turned her back to him and made her way more quickly down the aisle. 'Yes, I'll just bet you would.'

He laughed. 'Do I detect a touch of irritation in that soft voice? You're really going to have to work on that temper, sweetheart. It won't go over very well in the circles you hope to move in.'

'Listen,' Arden said, whirling to face him, 'if I want advice——'

The words caught in her throat. Turning so quickly hadn't been a good idea. He'd been right behind her, closer than she'd realised. Swinging around had brought them face to face or, rather, face to chest. Her nose was inches from that tightly pulled T-shirt; she caught a sudden whiff of the aroma of the stallion mixed with Conor's particular masculine scent, felt the heat emanating from his body.

A primal desire spread through her body with the swiftness of lightning; she swayed unsteadily and Conor caught her by the shoulders. Their eyes met, and suddenly she felt as if the ground were opening beneath her, as if any movement or mis-step would send her tumbling into oblivion.

She took a breath. 'You were going to tell me about the horses,' she said, her voice as cool as winter.

The muscle in Conor's cheek twitched. 'Yes,' he said, after a moment. He brushed past her. 'We raise Arabians,' he said in a businesslike, almost brusque manner. 'We did have Morgans, at one time, but the Arabians did better in this climate and so we——'

'We?' Arden's lips curved into a tight smile. 'Don't you mean "Felix"?'

'I mean precisely what I said. I have time and money invested in El Corazon, Arden, a great deal of both.'

'And you'll be damned if you don't get the return you expect.'

The horse nearest them whinnied and Conor reached out and patted its arched neck.

'You'll have to watch your language, too,' he said. 'Temper, language——' He shook his head. 'I don't know, sweetheart. Can you redo yourself, do you think?'

'I have no wish to "redo" myself,' she said angrily.

'I don't know if the moneyed crowd will hold it against you. I mean, after all, you're a *gringa*, but——'

Arden stamped her foot. 'I *hate* the way you say that!'

'Why?' He swung towards her, smiling. 'It's true, isn't it?'

'Yes, but you make it sound as if—as if being North American is something I ought to apologise for.'

He laughed, showing even white teeth. 'Have I asked for an apology?'

'I didn't mean it that way and you know it. I only meant...' Arden blew out her breath. 'Why does it give you such pleasure to insult me?'

His smile faded and his gaze swept over her, lingering on the thrust of her breasts and then on her lips.

'Is that what you think?'

'You've thought heaven only knows what about me from the beginning, and I resent it!'

Conor gave her a long look and then he smiled tightly. 'Perhaps you're right.' He turned and began walking slowly down the aisle. 'As I said, our stock is primarily Arabian. The current count stands at eight stallions, twenty-four mares, and half a dozen foals...'

Arden followed blindly after him, listening as his voice droned on but not hearing the words. Why had she said that? She'd made a point of never defending herself to him, not after that first ugly night. Then why...?

'If I'm boring you, just say so.'

She blinked. Conor was standing facing her, his hands on his hips, his mouth narrow.

'No,' she said quickly, 'no, you're not. I don't know anything about horses, just how to ride a bit.'

'Yes, I'm sure you made a point of learning that.' His eyes were like chips of green ice. 'Riding is a way of life here, on the *finca*, but I suppose it's a sort of a prerequisite for the life you prefer.'

Arden's eyes flashed as dangerously as his. 'I don't suppose it would ever occur to you that I simply like to ride.'

He smiled tightly. 'You're right. It wouldn't.'

'I hate to disappoint you,' she said with a toss of her head, 'but I do.'

'What do you like best about it, hmm? The people you meet? The Hunt Club balls? Come on, Arden, this is me, remember? I know the truth about you.'

'If you did, you'd know that the last thing I'd want to do is go to a ball——'

'Why?' Conor's smile was sly. 'Wouldn't the wealthy old gentleman who paid for your lessons pay for the gowns you'd need?'

'I paid for my own lessons,' she snapped, jabbing her forefinger against her breast. 'I paid by mucking out stalls—— '

'Why?'

'What do you mean, why? Because I wanted to ride, that's why! Because riding meant getting away by myself, into the woods where it was quiet, where no one looked at you and judged you by whether you lived on the Hill or in the valley, because sometimes I got tired of watching my mother wait hand and foot on other people...'

She fell silent, shocked as much by everything she'd said to him as by the fact that she'd needed to say it.

'That's not a great way to grow up.'

Arden looked up sharply, searching Conor's face for some hint of sarcasm, but she found none. She sighed.

'It wasn't,' she said. 'I mean, when I look back I realise that it was—it was just that my mother worked so hard for everything she had...' Her chin lifted defiantly. 'And so have I.'

A long moment seemed to pass. When Conor finally spoke, there was an abrasiveness to his voice Arden had never heard before.

'How hard did you work for that money Lithgow sent to your hotel room?'

'God, but you're all so damned predictable!'

She swung away, but Conor reached out and caught her wrist.

'It's not a tough question, Arden. Surely, you can answer it. How hard did you work for——'

'That was my severance pay!' She swiveled towards him, her eyes blazing. 'Lithgow left town before he authorised the office to give it to me. That was why I had to come to work here, for Felix. When I went back to confront him, he promised to make good on what he owed me.'

'And so he sent you an envelope filled with cash.' Conor's mouth twisted. 'Come on, sweetheart, you can come up with a better story than that!'

'It's the truth, dammit! I was angry because my cheque hadn't come in. I guess he decided to lay out the money himself and...' Arden puffed out her breath. 'I don't owe you any explanations, Conor!'

They stood staring at each other, both of them breathing heavily, and then Conor nodded.

'You're right,' he said slowly. His fingers flexed; his hand fell away from her wrist. There was a silence, and then he cleared his throat. 'I was telling you about the horses,' he said. 'We have eight stallions, two dozen mares, six foals, and eight geldings.' He reached out and rubbed the ear of the horse in the last stall and the animal nickered softly in response. 'Although we may be adding to that number, unfortunately. One of the stallions has been a problem lately, and——'

'And you'd geld him, just for that?'

'It's not pleasant, but we may have no choice. Diablo is half crazy with the scent of one of the mares. All he can think about is covering her. He's become a danger to himself and to others.'

Arden swallowed hard. 'Can't you—can't you solve the problem by letting him... by letting him...'

What was the matter with her? They were discussing horses, not people, and she'd spent enough time around horses to know that people who bred them discussed the sex lives of the animals as if they were discussing the propagation of cabbages.

But there was something dark and deep in Conor's words, just as there was in the way he was looking at her and in the way she was beginning to find it hard to breathe.

'By letting him take her?' he said. Arden nodded. 'I've tried that,' he said, very softly. 'But she won't accept him. He's too wild and untamed. Soon, he'll be dangerous. The passion that drives him makes him unfit for anything else.'

'Well, then,' she said carefully, 'whatever you think has to be done...'

Conor looked at her for a long minute and then he laughed.

'I half expected you to tell me what *you* thought needs to be done. I mean, now that you think you've a claim on the ranch——'

'Think? I don't "think", Conor, I know! I *have* a claim on the ranch.'

'Which is why you came strolling down to the stables to check things out first hand.'

'I told you, I came to saddle a horse and go riding.'

'Ah.' He shifted lazily and tucked his hands into the back pockets of his jeans. 'You thought you'd kill two birds with one stone, make an inventory of the stock we own, and see the *finca* close up, all at the same time.'

Arden's brows lifted. '*We* don't own anything.'

'I was trying to be polite. But you're right: it's better to be honest.' His smile tightened. 'I own it all.'

'Keep on dreaming, if it makes you happy.'

'You're in for one hell of a disappointment, sweetheart. El Corazon will never belong to anyone but me.'

'According to your uncle's will——'

'I'd advise you to remember that nothing will change on this *finca* while the will is in probate. For the past five years, I've made all the decisions here.'

'Yes, I'll just bet you have!'

'Is there some deep meaning in that remark?'

Arden shrugged her shoulders. 'Felix told me how determined you were to push him aside and take over.'

'Did he,' he said, in a way that made the words a statement, not a question.

'Felix was old, but he wasn't a fool. He knew what you wanted——'

'—and you helped him find a way to keep me from getting it.' His eyes bored into hers. 'How generous of you, Arden.'

'If you're implying that I suggested he leave the ranch to me——'

'I'd rather a court made that determination.'

'That's ridiculous! I told you, Felix and I never discussed El Corazon or what should be done with it.'

'No?'

'No!'

He smiled coolly. 'But you just said you did.'

'Wipe that smug look from your face, Conor! Felix told me you wanted to snatch the ranch from him. End of story.'

'Did it ever occur to you to ask me my plans for El Corazon instead of swallowing Felix's story intact?'

'Are you telling me he was lying?'

'I'm not telling you anything, for God's sake!'

Arden laughed in his face. 'Who's got a foul mouth now?'

Conor reached out and grabbed her. 'You'll drive me to more than profanity, if you're not careful!'

'Get out of my way, Conor.'

His jaw tightened. 'Where are you going?'

'That's none of your business!'

'It's my business if you're going to sashay around my stables.'

Arden laughed incredulously. 'I don't believe you! We just talked about whose property this is, and still you have the nerve to——'

'El Corazon is still in my possession. And possession is nine-tenths of the law.'

'You can't possess what you don't own.'

He took his hands from his back pockets suddenly, and she fell back. Her shoulders hit the wall and the atmosphere crackled with tension.

'Shall I prove my possession to you, Arden?'

Her heart kicked against her ribs, but when she spoke, her voice was cool and controlled.

'I should have known. When discussion fails, try intimidation.'

His smile softened, grew sexy and dangerous. 'Intimidation? Is that what you call this?'

'What would you call it?'

He laughed softly. 'I'm sure we can come up with a name, if we try hard enough.'

'Stop it,' she said sharply. 'I'm not in the mood for...'

'You've been in the mood for this from day one,' he said softly, taking hold of her shoulders.

'You bastard! You don't——'

His mouth dropped to hers, cutting off the rest of her words. His kiss was expert and sensual, the kiss of a man accustomed to winning response from a willing woman, but Arden wasn't willing. He drew back.

'Go on, play hard to get.' He smiled. 'A little make-believe can be fun.'

'Let go of me,' she said coldly.

'You don't really want me to do that.'

'You haven't any idea what I want or don't want!'

'Haven't I?'

'No! You think—you're so damned certain that I...'

Suddenly, to Arden's dismay, tears rose in her eyes. She tried blinking them back but it was impossible; she felt them roll down her cheeks and she stared at Conor in horror, hating herself for this unexpected show of weakness, hating him for somehow bringing it on. She had not cried once throughout this whole hideous ordeal, not when Edgar Lithgow had attacked her, not when Conor had degraded her, not even when she'd found herself adrift in a strange country.

Conor drew in his breath. 'Why are you crying?'

'I'm not! I never cry!'

His thumbs lifted, skimmed her cheeks, smudging the tears against her skin.

'No?' he said softly. 'What do you call this, then?'

'Stupidity.' The tears came harder and she closed her eyes. 'All right, Conor, make the most of this moment. I promise you, you'll never see me cry again.'

'Hell,' he said again, his voice rough. He took her face in his hands and lifted it to him. 'I didn't mean to make you cry. I only wanted to—I only wanted to——' His gaze dropped to her mouth. 'I only wanted to kiss you,' he whispered, and he bent to her, his mouth unrelenting in its search for hers and incredibly, indescribably tender in its capture.

There were a thousand reasons to deny him, a thousand more to pound her fists against his chest and tear free of the arms that were encircling her. But she did neither. A sweet, fierce flame burst to life deep within her; she gave a sob of acquiescence, rose on her toes, and wound her arms tightly around Conor's neck.

He groaned her name and gathered her closer, kissing her again and again. Her breasts flattened against his chest, her thighs moulded to his, their heartbeats merged and became one swift, galloping race of desire.

Arden put her hands into Conor's hair, curling her fingers into that dark silk she had so longed to touch. What was the point in denying it now? He was right. She had wanted this for days, for weeks, perhaps for a lifetime, she'd wanted to touch him, to be touched by him, to hold him in her arms and feel his passion, know he wanted her.

It was impossible to get close enough to him. She wanted to feel every inch of his flesh against hers, she wanted to touch him everywhere and be touched in return.

It was as if Conor had read her thoughts. He shifted his weight and all at once she felt the hardness of his arousal press against her. Heat bloomed deep in her belly and filled her with desire. The sweetness of the kiss became the fire of passion.

Conor's fingers tunnelled into her hair, tugged her head back. His teeth nipped sharply at her bottom lip and she made a little sound of pleasure and opened her mouth to him. He whispered against her lips, words in Spanish that needed no translation. His hands slipped to her buttocks and he lifted her into the pulsing thrust of his erection.

'*Querida*,' he murmured, '*querida mia ...*'

His hands were under her T-shirt, tugging it impatiently from her jeans; his mouth was at her throat. He fumbled at the front closure of her bra and then her breasts were naked in his hands. She cried out as his thumbs skimmed across her nipples, cried out again as a flooding pool of warmth and dampness welled between her thighs.

'Conor,' she said desperately, as if the answer to what was happening to her might be contained in that one word, 'Conor...'

'*Cuidado*!'

The warning cry sliced the air like the crack of a whip. Arden's eyes flew open. She heard the beat of powerful hoofs and then the sound of her own scream as a huge black stallion came thundering down the aisle towards them, its breath hot and its eyes rolling.

Conor lunged for the animal's halter, and the beast reared up on its hind legs, slashing at the air with razor-sharp hooves.

'Conor,' she screamed, and he thrust her behind him. The back of her skull thunked hard against the stable wall.

After that, there was only darkness.

CHAPTER NINE

ARDEN had never passed out in her life. What she knew about such things came from films and books. Women fainted, then returned to consciousness with a sort of genteel grace.

But fiction, it seemed, had little to do with real life. One moment she was submerged in a sea of darkness and the next, she was rushing up through that sea towards a blinding light while an urgent voice repeated her name endlessly.

Her eyelids felt heavy but she forced them open and focused her vision on a face looking down at her. It was Conor, but Conor as she had never seen him, with his skin drawn tight over his cheekbones and his eyes as dark as the darkest jade.

'Conor?' she said in a shaky whisper.

A long, slow exhalation of pent-up breath whistled from his lungs and he smiled.

'It's all right,' he murmured. 'It's all right, *querida* You're fine.'

Was she? Her head hurt a little, but she couldn't remember why any more than she could understand the reason she was lying here, tightly held in Conor's encircling arms. She only knew that there was comfort in those arms, comfort and a peace she had never known before.

She ran her tongue over her lips. 'What—what happened?'

'You hit your head against the wall and knocked yourself out.'

Arden frowned. 'Did I? I don't remember...'

And then she did. The horse, the huge black horse, coming suddenly from out of the shadows, its hoofs slashing down like razors; Conor, shoving her behind him to safety; Conor, facing the animal's fierce rage alone...

'The horse,' she said frantically as she struggled to get up, 'oh, God, the horse...'

Conor's arms tightened around her. He held her closer, whispering soothing words in Spanish, rubbing her back gently, as if she were a frightened child.

'It's over, *querida*,' he said quietly. 'You're safe now. Diablo's safely locked away.'

'Are you all right?' She drew back, enough so she could look searchingly into his face. 'Did he hurt you?'

He smiled a little. 'No, no, I'm fine. The horse broke loose from the boy who was taking him back to his stall, but he's safely locked away now.'

Arden sighed, closed her eyes, and let Conor's gentle hands go on stroking the tension from her body.

'Good,' she whispered.

'Arden.' His hand cupped her cheek and she opened her eyes and looked at him. 'Don't drift off again, *querida*. You might have a concussion.'

'I don't think so. I can see OK, and I'm not nauseous or anything...' She winced as she sat up a little. 'My head hurts, though.' Her breath caught as she touched her fingers lightly to the back of her skull. 'And I've got a lump here, but——'

'Let me see.' Conor leaned forward, his fingers dancing over hers. 'Yes, I see it. It's not bleeding, but I'll take a better look when we get to the house.'

She nodded. The simple action sent a dull pain rocketing through her skull and she made a little sound of distress.

'Easy, *querida*.' Conor shifted her in his arms. 'A couple of aspirin and an ice-pack will make you feel better while we wait for the doctor.'

'Don't be silly. I don't need a doc—— What are you doing?'

'What does it look as if I'm doing?' he said as he scooped her up and rose to his feet.

'I can walk!'

'I'm sure you can.' He strode to the stable door and shouldered it open. 'But I'm not taking any chances until I've checked you over more thoroughly.'

'Conor, really, I'm perfectly fine. You don't have to carry me.'

He glanced down at her. 'I don't,' he said in a tone that she recognised all too well, a tone that said Conor Martinez was in charge and everyone else had better stay out of the way. 'But I'm going to.' He smiled a little in a way that softened the hard-edged command. 'Why don't you just enjoy the ride, *querida*?'

She stared into his eyes. They had gone back to the colour of emeralds again, although now that her face was only inches from his she could see that the irises were flecked with gold.

'Arden.' His voice was soft. 'Put your arms around my neck, OK?'

It was such a simple suggestion, but the intimacy in the way he was holding her would somehow be heightened when she looped her arms around him. It was easy, breathtakingly easy, to imagine him carrying her not to her room but to some soft, secret corner of the garden where he would make love to her for hours and hours.

'Arden?'

His mouth was only inches from hers. A tremor went through her. Yes, she thought, oh, yes...

She swallowed hard, then did as he'd asked. Conor nodded.

'Good girl.'

His stride was long and steady; he carried her as if she were weightless. And it felt—it felt wonderful to be in his arms this way, to feel the steady beat of his heart against hers, to smell the early-morning scents of soap, man, and horse, to feel the warmth of his body under her hands.

Her heart gave an unsteady thump. Conor glanced down at her and smiled in a way that made her foolish heart skip a beat again.

'Don't worry,' he whispered. 'You'll be fine, *querida*. I would never let anything happen to you.'

But something had already happened to her, and he was the cause of it. Conor was—he was——

Arden screwed her eyes shut. No. No, she wouldn't think that way.

'*Querida*?' Her eyes flew open. 'What's wrong? Are you feeling ill?'

Dumbly, she shook her head, then buried her face in Conor's shoulder as the room tilted. He muttered something harsh and his arms tightened around her as he strode into the house.

'Inez!' he roared.

The housekeeper came scurrying into the foyer, drying her hands on a kitchen towel. Her dark eyes widened as she took in the scene before her.

'We need two aspirin. And an icepack,' Conor barked in Spanish as he mounted the stairs. 'And phone for the *medico*. Tell him to come at once!'

Arden's room was cool and shadowed, the blinds and curtains drawn against the ascending sun. Conor carried her to the bed, sat her down gently and held her in the curve of his arm while he plumped the pillows behind

her. Then he eased her back against them and switched
on the bedside lamp just as Inez came bustling in with
a glass of water, a packet of aspirin, and an ice pack.

'*Gracias*, Inez. Now,' Conor said, 'let's get a better
look at that bump.' He clasped Arden's shoulders, drew
her towards him until her head was against his chest.
Arden closed her eyes and listened to the steady beat of
his heart as he carefully parted her hair with his fingertips, then stroked lightly over the swelling on her skull.
'Does that hurt?'

It did, a little. But being in his arms more than com-
pensated for the discomfort. His touch was soft and
tender, and suddenly she recalled how he'd touched her
moments before the accident, his hands moving across
her bare breasts and arousing her to hot, honeyed
passion...

She scooted back against the pillows. 'Honestly,' she
said with a shaky laugh, 'I'll be fine.'

'I'm sure you're right.' Conor smiled. 'But we'll let
the doctor make it official.'

'No,' Arden said quickly. 'I don't need a doctor,
Conor. If you'd just——' If you'd just leave me alone,
before I make a fool of myself, she thought shakily, but
that wasn't what she said. 'If you'd just let me get some
rest——'

'Not until after the doctor's checked you over.'
Frowning, he leaned towards her and framed her face
with his hands. 'Let me see your eyes.'

'My eyes?' she repeated foolishly as his face drew level
with hers.

'One of the ways you check for concussion is by seeing
how the pupils react to light. Look towards the lamp,
please.'

'Conor, really, my eyes are fine——'

'They're not fine.'

'But they are. They're——'

'They're beautiful.' Her eyes flashed to his. He was frowning, as if he'd just seen something he'd never seen before. 'I just—I just can't decide if they're hazel or...' Their eyes met and a dark flush rose along Conor's high cheekbones. He cleared his throat and got to his feet. 'Well,' he said briskly, 'why don't I open these blinds a little?'

Arden swallowed. 'Fine,' she said shakily. She shut her eyes. 'That's—that's a good——'

'Don't close your eyes!' Her lashes flew up from her cheeks and she stared at him. 'Remember what I said? I don't want you to doze off until the doctor's seen you.'

'Yes, but——'

'Are you sleepy?'

She wasn't. She just didn't want him to look into her eyes again, for if he did—if he did, who knew what he might see?

Conor sat down on the bed beside her. 'Talk to me, Arden, and keep yourself awake.'

She gave a helpless laugh. 'Talk to you? About what?'

'I don't know. Anything.' He grinned. 'Tell me about the little girl who mucked stables in her spare time. What did she like, besides horses?'

'This is silly. I'm——'

'Did she play with dolls and colouring books? Or was she a tomboy who was always coming home with dirty knees and bruises on her shins?'

Arden smiled a little. 'A tomboy. My mother bought me a doll each Christmas, in hopes I'd turn into the demure child she wanted.'

His grin widened. 'But it didn't work.'

'Uh-uh. I never understood why any girl in her right mind would want to pour tea for her dolls when she could be out tramping through the woods or——'

'Or riding a horse,' he said, taking her hand in his, 'so she could get away from all those insensitive bastards who never let her forget she was the daughter of a servant.'

Arden's smile vanished. She tried to tug her hand free of his, but he wouldn't let her do it.

'I don't know why I told you that,' she said.

'Perhaps because you wanted me to understand you better.'

Colour stained her cheeks. 'If you think I was asking you for your pity——'

'Did I say that, *querida*?'

'No,' she said, after a second, 'you didn't. But——'

'And I do understand you better now. You see, I grew up much the same way.'

Arden smiled cynically. 'Who are you trying to kid, Conor? You grew up in this big house——'

'—in this big house, with an uncle who rarely let a day pass without somehow reminding me that he'd taken me in, and I was obliged to him.'

Her smile faded. 'Felix?'

Conor looked down at where her hand lay in his. 'I don't really blame him now,' he said slowly. 'He didn't know the first thing about children and all of a sudden, there he was, a man in his seventies, with a boy to raise.'

Arden looked at him. 'And so you rebelled,' she said softly. 'Is that why you worked on that banana boat?'

He smiled as he rubbed his fingers lightly over the back of her hand. 'Sort of. When I turned eighteen, he told me I could finally begin earning my keep. He put me to work here, at El Corazon. But having him bark orders at me twenty-four hours a day was even worse than having him constantly reminding me that I owed him everything. One day, I decided it was impossible for me to live *my* life so *he* could be happy. I packed a change of clothing and left.'

'But you came back,' he said quietly.

Conor shrugged. 'Eventually.'

'Then, you must have had some good memories of the years you spent here.'

He smiled slightly. 'Do you have good memories of— what's the name of that town in Connecticut?'

'Greenfield.' She hesitated, then smiled back at him. 'Of course. Nothing's ever completely black or white.'

'Exactly. Besides, I had to come back. Felix was sick.'

'He told me.' Arden paused again. 'He said you came back to the ranch to take it away from him.'

'Did he?' Conor said, with a quick, flat smile. 'Yes, it's the way he'd think, that I wanted to avenge the injustice he did my father. And he wasn't wrong, Arden, he——'

'Señor Martinez?' The rap at the door, and the voice, came at the same instant. Arden looked up as a portly man carrying a small black bag stepped into the room.

'Dr Borgas.' Conor rose, his hand extended. 'Thank you for coming so promptly.' He nodded towards Arden. 'This is Señorita Miller. She's had a bump on the head, and I'd be most grateful if you'd examine her and see if she's all right.'

Arden made a face. 'I'm fine,' she said. 'Really. I had a headache, but even that's gone now.'

'Let me be the judge of that, *señorita*.' He looked at Conor. 'If you will be good enough to leave us, *señor*...?'

Conor did, but only after frowning and assuring Arden that he would be just outside if she should need him. Borgas smiled as the door shut after him.

'Señor Martinez is very protective of you, *señorita*.'

Arden flushed. 'Oh, no, Doctor. He's just concerned about my injury.'

'As you prefer. Still,' he said, with a little smile, 'I would prefer to examine you so that I may assure the *señor* that you are fine and healthy and he need not wear out the hallway, pacing it as he worries about you. Lie back, please, Señorita Miller, and look directly at this light.'

It took less than half an hour for the doctor to confirm Arden's self-diagnosis. She was fine, except for the lump on her head.

'Are you certain?' Conor demanded, when he was let back into the room for the diagnosis.

'Quite certain,' Borgas said with a smile. 'Just see to it the *señorita* rests for the balance of the day and for the evening. Tomorrow, her life can return to normal.'

Arden awoke to a soft rap at the door the next morning. Inez, she thought groggily, come to bring her a breakfast tray, just as she had brought her lunch and dinner yesterday, at Conor's insistence.

Arden sighed and sat up against the pillows. Conor had obviously forgotten Dr Borgas's instructions. Breakfast in bed was hardly 'normal'.

Well, she'd put a stop to that immediately.

'Come in,' she called as she tossed back the blankets. The door opened and she looked up, shaking her head and smiling. 'Inez, you take that tray right back to the . . . Conor.' She blinked foolishly, then snatched the blanket and drew it up to her chin. 'What are you doing here?'

He smiled at her, tall and ruggedly handsome in jeans and a faded denim shirt.

'Good morning, *querida* How do you feel today?'

'Fine, thank you. But——'

'Fine enough to breakfast *al fresco*?'

She smiled uncertainly. 'To what?'

'I thought we'd have our coffee outside today.'

'On the terrace?'

He grinned. 'Better than that.'

'I don't understand... ?'

'Are you up to a ride in—what did you call it?—in my "old Jeep"?'

She flushed. 'In the Bronco?'

'I promise,' he said with an engaging grin, 'this time I won't aim for every pothole.'

Arden couldn't help laughing. 'So, you admit it.'

Conor laughed, too, but then his smile faded and his eyes turned dark and smoky.

'Well?' he said softly. 'What do you say? Will you come with me, *querida*?'

Her heartbeat quickened and a danger signal began to flash into her brain, but nothing could stop him from the answer she gave him.

'Yes,' Arden whispered. 'I will.'

The *finca* was enormous, she had known that. Felix had told her it stretched in all directions for thousands and thousands of acres, but seeing all that land, driving through it, made the size of it real in a way numbers scratched on paper never could.

Conor tucked her into the Bronco as carefully as if she were made of glass, loaded a picnic hamper into the rear, then drove them first to the top of a ridge where they sat looking over a field of wild flowers, drinking a Thermos of dark, sweet coffee and munching on fresh cinnamon rolls.

'I want to show you the rest of the *finca*,' Conor said, after they'd got back into the car, 'but first, if you're up to it, I thought I'd take you to the most beautiful place I know.'

Arden smiled. 'Prettier than the lake?'

'Yes.'

She lay her head back and sighed. 'Then it has a lot to live up to, Conor, I'm warning you.'

He grinned. 'Is that a yes?'

'Uh huh.'

He turned the key and the Bronco lurched forward. 'Just promise you'll tell me if I'm driving too fast. Or if your head hurts. Or——'

'Conor, honestly, I'm fine.'

'You're sure?'

She smiled at him. 'Positive.'

And she was, she thought as they drove along a narrow dirt road that wound into the hills; she was finer than she had ever been before.

Her gaze flew to the man beside her. It was wrong, that she should feel so happy to be with him. Conor was the enemy—although it was getting harder and harder to remember that. Where was the river of anger that had flowed between them the past weeks? Had such a simple thing as a runaway horse, a blow to the head, turned it back—or had there been something other than anger driving her all along? Had despising Conor been safer than—than——?

'Why so quiet?'

Arden blinked. Conor was looking at her, a questioning smile on his face.

'I—I was just—just thinking how lovely El Corazon is.' She bit her lip. 'And—and how big it is...'

She broke off, wishing she could call back the words, certain Conor would interpret them to mean she was weighing and measuring the monetary worth of the ranch that had been willed her, but he only smiled.

'Bigger than you realise, *querida*. And what we're about to see is the most beautiful part of it.' He shut off the engine and the silence of the forest enfolded them.

'Are you up to a five-minute walk?' Arden nodded, and Conor stepped from the Bronco, came around to her side, and lifted her gently down. He took her hand and led her along a narrow path that wound into a dense stand of magnificent trees.

'What is this place?' she asked softly.

Conor smiled. 'The cloud forest.'

'The cloud forest.' She shivered with delight. 'What a wonderful name! It sounds magical.'

'Look up, past the tops of the trees, and you'll see why it's called that.'

He slipped his arm around her waist and she tilted her head back, watching the clouds that rode the sky so low it seemed they might catch in the branches of the trees.

'El Corazon boundaries encompass only a small portion of the forest.' He grinned as he took her hand again and led her further along the path. 'The first time I stood up to Felix was over those few hundred acres.'

'What do you mean?'

'He had an offer to sell them. An extraordinarily good offer, as I recall.'

'To whom?'

'To a company that makes furniture of what they call "exotic woods".'

'And you stopped him? How?'

Conor smiled. 'By threatening to contact the Friends of the Forest and every other environmental organisation I could find. He laughed in my face—until I pointed out that every last one of them would take him to court and it would cost him thousands upon thousands of dollars to defend himself.'

Arden laughed. 'Good thinking.'

'It wasn't an empty threat. The legal profession can be like an evil juggernaut, destroying everything and everyone that gets in its path. The only people who profit are attorneys.'

'So,' she said, 'you saved the cloud forest.'

'Only a small piece of it,' he said, twining his fingers through hers, 'but, I must admit, an exceptionally beautiful piece. See for yourself.'

He stepped back so that she could move out ahead of him. She walked forward another few paces, then caught her breath. The dense wall of green had given way to a small clearing bordered by ancient oaks and tall palms, patched with vines and wild flowers, and bisected by a stream that tumbled down from the mountain.

'You were right.' Arden swung around to face Conor. 'It is beautiful, Conor. It's perfect.'

'Yes,' he said, very softly. 'You're right, *querida*.' He reached out and stroked her hair back from her face. He smiled slightly, and his gaze fell to her mouth. 'I have never seen anything more perfect than this.'

Electricity danced along her skin. 'Conor,' she said in an urgent whisper, 'I don't think we——'

He took her face in his hands. 'You have the face of a madonna, Arden. Have I told you that?'

'We should talk,' she said shakily. 'We—we've had so many misconceptions about each other, and——'

'Do you remember what I said to you about what we should have done the night we met, *querida*?' He bent and brushed his lips against hers. 'If we had made love that night, there would have been no misconceptions. We would have known each other as we were meant to know each other from the day the world began.'

'Conor,' Arden whispered, 'Conor, I think——'

'I'll tell you what I think,' he said. He tilted her face to his and kissed her hungrily. 'I think,' he murmured, his mouth a flame against hers, 'that I will die if I don't touch your breasts again, that I must taste the silk of

your skin . . .' Her head fell back as he kissed her throat.
'My blood beats out your name with each beat of my
heart, Arden. I lie sleepless at night, imagining you naked
and on fire in my arms, thinking of how you'll tremble
beneath me . . .' Arden moaned softly, swayed forward,
and Conor caught her up in his arms. 'Tell me you want
me with that same passion,' he demanded. 'I want to
hear you say it.'

She looked into his eyes. How could she deny him
this, when it was what she yearned for, too? She wanted
him, she had always wanted him, and everything else—
the anger, the quarrels—had not diminished the wanting,
had even, in some strange way, intensified it.

'Tell me,' Conor said.

Arden sighed her surrender, put her arms around his
neck, and pressed her lips to his throat.

'I want you more than life itself,' she whispered.

He gave a growl of triumph and his mouth dropped
to hers, slanting over it hungrily as he carried her across
the little clearing to a velvety bed of emerald moss that
felt soft as feathers beneath her, and he came down
beside her. She put her hands against his chest, the palms
flattened so that the heavy beat of his heart thudded
under her touch, and he bent and kissed her deeply, his
tongue in her mouth, his hands driving deep into her
hair.

'You are more beautiful than any dream,' he murmured. His hand slipped across her cotton T-shirt,
tracing the outline of her breast, feathering lightly against
her thrusting nipple, and she caught his wrist, cupped
his hand to her flesh and held it there.

'Undress me,' she whispered.

His eyes turned to green flame. He took her hands,
kissed her wrists, her palms, then drew her up and
stripped off her shirt and bra, and her breasts fell free.

'So perfect, *querida*' he said, his voice a broken whisper. He cupped her breasts in his hands, lowered his face to them, moving his cheek over first one sensitive peak and then the other. The faint shadow of his beard lay just beneath his skin; the abrasive feel of it against her nipples was exquisite. Arden moaned softly. 'Shall I kiss your breasts, *querida*?' he said, and slowly, slowly, he lowered his head until she felt the warmth of his breath against her skin. The first touch of his tongue made her cry out, and when his mouth closed around the aroused centre she felt her soul burst free.

'Conor,' she said, the word a little sob. Her hands trembled as she slid them under his shirt. She heard the sharp hiss of his breath as she touched his hot skin, and then he drew back and yanked the shirt over his head and tossed it aside.

'Now, touch me,' he said fiercely, and she did, her fingers tracing the dark hair that whorled over his muscled chest, her mouth tasting his nipples as he had tasted hers. He whispered something, first in Spanish, then in English, something that turned her cheeks to flame.

'Yes,' she said, 'Oh, yes.'

Quickly, he stripped off the rest of her clothing, and then he lay her back against the grass and looked at her.

'I've waited so long to see you, Arden.' His voice was husky and thick. He reached out and ran his hand lightly along her body, from her throat to her breasts, across her belly and down to the soft, feminine delta between her thighs. His fingers dipped into the warm, moist darkness and the breath hissed from his lips. 'I want you,' he whispered, 'I want you so much——'

'Then take me,' she said. She saw the change her soft plea brought to his face, saw the sudden tightening of his mouth, the darkening of his eyes, and her body tightened in anticipation. 'Conor,' she whispered, and she held out her arms to him.

He rose and stripped off his clothing. Arden's breathing quickened when she saw how perfect he was, how magnificently and proudly male.

'You're beautiful,' she said, and then her voice broke. 'Please,' she sighed, 'Conor, please...'

He knelt above her, bent, kissed her mouth until it was as soft and swollen as a rose bud beneath his.

'Arden,' he said, '*mi amor.*'

She clasped his face and drew him to her. His mouth covered hers again; he kissed her, nibbled at her bottom lip, then stroked it with his tongue, and then, whispering her name, he thrust deep into her.

Arden cried out, not with pain but with the joy of fulfilment. Conor hesitated, his maleness still sheathed inside her, and looked down into her eyes.

'You are mine now, *querida,*' he said fiercely, and just before he began to move within her, before that moment when she shattered and became a million spinning suns, Arden knew, with wrenching certainty, that he was more right than he could possibly know, for the simple truth was that she loved Conor Martinez with all her heart and soul.

CHAPTER TEN

ARDEN took a brightly coloured ceramic mug from the dining-room sideboard, filled it with coffee, and added a dollop of cream. She strolled through the French doors to the glass-topped table that stood on the terrace and sat.

What a beautiful morning! she thought, with a smile of pleasure. Her smile deepened. That was nothing unusual, of course. Mornings in this part of Costa Rica, especially at this time of the year, were invariably lovely, but lately there was a special buttery cast to the sunlight, a soft perfume to the breeze. Was it because the seasons were changing? The dry months of summer were ending, and the rainy days of winter were fast approaching. She would have to ask Conor if that was the reason for the difference, have to ask him, too, if the shifting seasons were responsible for the sudden, unbelievable variety of butterflies she saw everywhere she looked, their wings iridescent and glinting with all the wondrous colour of the rainbow.

Two warm, strong hands dropped to her shoulders and clasped them tightly.

'Good morning,' a deep voice whispered. 'Did you sleep well, *querida*?'

Arden looked up. Conor was standing just behind her, smiling. With a swift, almost fierce joy she realised that it wasn't the weather that was changing, it was she. With each passing day, she fell more deeply in love with this man who had once been her hated enemy. That was the reason the sun seemed brighter, the creatures more exotic, because she had been caught up in a love so intense it made everything else all the more wonderful, but there was no way to tell him all that, not without giving him even more of her heart than he'd already taken, for Conor had not yet said he loved her.

The bittersweet realisation made her answering smile tremble on her lips as she put her hands over his.

'You know I did,' she whispered.

His smile tilted. He bent, kissed her mouth, then came around the table and sat in the chair opposite her.

'It was hard to leave you this morning, *querida*,' he said softly. He took her hand, lifted it to his lips, and kissed the palm. 'I wanted to stay with you, make love to you one last time before the day began.'

Arden flushed. 'But you did, don't you remember? You kissed me awake, and then——'

He smiled when she hesitated. 'Yes, sweetheart, I do remember. But there was still another hour until dawn.'

'Conor, I know you think I'm silly, asking you to leave my room before anyone's awake, but—but you know how I feel. I'd be embarrassed if the servants thought— if they knew——'

He leaned forward and silenced her halting explanation with a kiss. 'It's not silly,' he said, his eyes on hers. 'It's old-fashioned and charming.'

And unexpected, she thought. She knew how surprised he'd been when she'd told him they couldn't share a bed. It was the day they'd become lovers, almost two weeks before. They'd stayed in the little clearing in the cloud forest for hours, lying in each other's arms, touching and kissing and talking about a million different things, and then Conor had made love to her again, so long and so passionately that it had seemed an eternity until she'd come tumbling back to earth again. Finally, as the sun painted the forest with vermilion, they climbed into the Bronco and headed back to the ranch.

Once inside the house, Conor had gathered her tightly into his arms and kissed her.

'I'm going to tell Inez to move your things into my room,' he said softly.

'No,' Arden said quickly, 'no, don't do that.'

Conor's eyes narrowed fractionally. 'Very well, *querida*. If you prefer to give her the instruction your-self——'

'You don't understand.' She pressed her hands lightly against his chest. 'I—I can't share a room with you.'

'What do you mean? Of course you can.'

'I'm telling you, I can't. If I did—if I did, everyone would know that—that...' She stumbled to an embarrassed silence.

'That we're lovers,' he said, his eyes on hers.

Arden nodded. 'Yes. Servants—servants talk, Conor, they talk about what people do, and—and they make judgements. The people they work for don't realise it, they—they seem to think servants are part of the furniture, but——'

'Is that how you think I treat Inez and the rest? As if they belonged to me?'

'No,' she said quickly, 'oh, no, I wasn't accusing you of...' She drew a deep breath and rested her forehead against his chin. 'I know it sounds crazy, but that's how I feel. Please don't try and change my mind.'

He gathered her even closer in his arms. 'All right, then, *querida*. We'll do it your way.' He lowered his head and brushed his lips gently over hers. 'I'll come to you in the darkness of the night and leave you before the sun rises.' A slow, sexy smile curved across his mouth. 'You won't object to that, will you?'

Arden hadn't trusted herself to answer. Instead, she'd touched her hand to his cheek and Conor had kissed her again, this time with slow, sweet care.

'Wanting you is like wanting a dozen different women,' he'd said while he held her. 'You're never quite what I expect you to be—and yet you're always what I want.'

Now, watching as he sipped his morning coffee, she thought of those whispered words and wondered, as she had many times during the past days, what he'd meant by them. She would want him forever, she knew that without question, but what did 'forever' mean to a man like Conor Martinez? Surely there had been women, perhaps lots of women, before her. No man who looked the way he did, who pleased a woman the way he could, would have lived the existence of a saint.

An even darker thought had come to her late last night, as she lay drowsing in Conor's arms. Listening to his slow, steady breathing, she'd suddenly wondered if his wanting her had anything to do with his wanting El Corazon.

But that was foolish. There'd been a fever of need between the two of them from the start, even though they'd both done their best to suppress it.

Besides, according to the lawyer she'd contacted, nothing either of them did now would—or could—change the will. Even if she'd wanted to renounce Felix's bequest, she couldn't. The *finca* was legally hers, at least, until the lawyers or the court decided otherwise.

She didn't want El Corazon, she thought suddenly. In her heart, she'd known that from the start. Hadn't she almost said that to Conor when she'd first learned of Felix's incredible bequest? But anger had kept her silent.

What Felix had done was wrong. And cruel. He'd given her the ranch not out of kindness but out of his desire to hurt Conor. She, too, was hurting him, denying

him El Corazon when, in truth, it should be his. He was
tied to the land by blood, by sweat, by love...

'Hey.' Conor was leaning towards her across the table,
his brow creased. He gave her a little smile, took her
hand, and brought it to his lips. 'Are you OK?'

She stared at him. Why had it taken her so long to
see the truth? But then, the truth had been a long time
coming to both of them about a lot of things. She had
lumped Conor in with the rich boys and men she'd grown
up despising, men who'd seen women like her as servants or playthings. Conor had been blind, too. He'd let
circumstance and a handful of lies convince him she was
a woman who preyed upon men.

Neither of them had mentioned the will since they'd
become lovers. She knew Conor must feel as she did,
afraid to allow the impossibility of the situation to intrude upon the fragile world they'd created. But she could
change all that. She had only to turn to Conor, to tell
him it was he who deserved El Corazon, that she would
make things right.

She smiled, laced her fingers through his, drew a deep
breath. She felt light, carefree, as if some awful burden
had been lifted from her shoulders.

'Conor,' she said, 'we have to talk.'

He laughed softly. 'Felix was right,' he said. 'You talk
more than any woman I've ever known.'

'It's Felix I want to talk about, Conor.
About——' She took a breath. 'About his will.'

His smile vanished instantly. 'No.'

'Yes.' Her hand tightened on his. 'We must.
We——'

'There's nothing to discuss, Arden.' His voice was taut,
almost cool, in a way it had not been in days.

'But there is. We can't keep pretending that—that El
Corazon's not—not——' Not mine, she'd almost said,

but the look in Conor's eyes made her swallow the word. 'That it's not lying between us,' she said unhappily.

Conor pushed back his chair and rose to his feet. 'We'll deal with what's between us when the time comes,' he said in the same tone. Arden could almost see him pulling himself together. Finally, he held his hand out to her. 'Now, have you forgotten, *querida*? We've a fiesta to attend.'

At this moment, that was the last thing she felt like doing. But Conor was standing over her, a strained smile on his lips, and for the first time she thought that it would be better to spend the day with lots of people than to spend it alone together. With a smile as artificial as his, Arden stood up and took his outstretched hand.

'It sounds like fun,' she said brightly, and she breathed a silent prayer that she'd be right.

The fiesta was being held in a town not more than half an hour's drive up the dirt road Arden had foolishly imagined ended past El Corazon's iron gates. Now, she knew that the road stretched on through the rainforest almost to the Pacific coast. There were villages on the road, Conor said as they rattled along, ones very much like the one they were going to.

'They're all small,' he said. 'Blink your eyes and you'd miss half of them.'

Ampara was one of the larger villages. Four straight streets, lined with red-roofed, white stucco houses, intersected in a square where an old mission church stood surrounded by palm trees. The town was alive with a happy, colourful fiesta crowd.

Except for an occasional comment about the road, Conor had said nothing during the drive, and when he pulled the Bronco under a tree at the end of town and shut off the ignition Arden was desperate to clear the air. When he came around to her side of the car and held out his arms to help her down, she hesitated.

'Conor,' she said as she put her hands on his shoulders, 'about the *finca*—I didn't mean to make you angry, I just——'

'I told you, I don't want to talk about it.'

'But——'

'Felix was right,' he said sharply. 'No *tica* would behave as you do.'

A little warning bell sounded inside her head. 'That's the second time this morning you've said that.'

'Said what?'

'That Felix was right about me.' Her eyes were steady on his. 'It doesn't sound much like a compliment.'

Conor stared up at her as she stood above him on the running board of the Bronco, his face expressionless, and then he blew out his breath. 'I'm sorry, *querida*. I didn't mean to hurt your feelings.'

'You haven't. It's just—I don't understand you, Conor. Why is it all right for you to bring up his name but not me? I know how you feel about Felix, about the will, I understand that it angers you to think about it, but——'

'Ah, that's wonderful,' Conor snapped. 'A little armchair analysis from the *gringa*. But you're wasting your time. You don't understand any of this, not in the slightest!'

Arden's face went tight-lipped with anger. 'You're right,' she hissed, slamming his shoulders with the heels of her hands. 'I don't understand you, not one bit, but then, how could I? You're a—a pig-headed fool, you're the worst combination of Irish stubbornness and Latin machismo that I ever——' Conor began to laugh. 'Stop that,' she demanded. 'Dammit, Conor, how dare you laugh at me?'

He swung her from the car, caught her face between his hands, and kissed her to silence. The anger drained out of her and a sweet languor filled her senses instead, so that when he finally lifted his mouth from hers, she felt boneless in his arms.

'I apologise again, *querida*,' he said softly. 'You're right, we do have to discuss our problem.' The muscle tightened in his cheek. 'Especially since Linda's coming back tomorrow.'

Arden's stomach clenched. In the happiness of the past days, she'd almost forgotten Linda. The girl had disliked her when she'd only been an employee at El Corazon. Heaven only knew how she'd react to her now that she was Felix's heir—and Conor's lover.

'Arden?' Their eyes met, and he smiled. 'I've been thinking about it a great deal, about Felix and the codicil and the ranch, and I've come up with a solution.'

'I have, too,' she said quickly. 'And——'

Conor brushed his mouth over hers. 'I don't want to talk about it here, sweetheart.'

A sigh escaped her lungs. 'All right,' she whispered. 'But as soon as we get back to the ranch——'

He kissed her again, even more sweetly, so that her heart was racing when they drew apart.

'I want so badly to be alone with you,' he said huskily. 'But first, I must pay my respects to the *alcalde*.' Conor looped his arm around Arden's shoulders and they began walking slowly towards the centre of town. 'The mayor is an old friend, and the party is for his daughter's tenth birthday.'

Arden began to smile. 'You mean, the whole town's turned out for a birthday party for a little girl?'

'Any excuse is a good one in my country. My people love to eat, to dance, to fight the bulls——'

'Here? Today?' She shook her head emphatically. 'I don't want to see that, Conor. I know it's very Spanish, I know that lots of people think it's noble and beautiful and poetic, but——' He began to laugh, and she glared at him. 'If you tell me one more time that I'm behaving like a *gringa*,' she said, 'I'll——'

'I'm laughing at your description of a Costa Rican bullfight,' he said, hugging her closer to him. 'Noble? Beautiful? Poetic? No. I don't think so, *querida*.'

'Whatever you call it, I'll hate it!'

'What's that North American expression? Something about putting your money where your mouth is?'

'There's no point in betting that I'll change my mind,' Arden said positively. 'I promise you, I won't.'

'In that case, what have you to lose? Let me take you to the fight. You can watch for five minutes and then we'll decide who wins the wager.'

'I'll watch for one minute. That's all it will take you to lose.'

'Agreed.' Conor stopped walking and swung her towards him. 'Now, what shall we wager?' He grinned. 'It should be something meaningful, don't you agree, *querida*?'

She could feel her breath catch. El Corazon, she thought, he was going to ask her to wager El Corazon...

'Something of great importance to the both of us.' He took her face in his hands and tilted it to his. 'What I suggest,' he whispered inches from her mouth, 'is one night in my bed.'

Arden's eyes rounded. 'What?'

'If you lose the wager, you must spend the night with me. The entire night, from just after dinner until it's time for breakfast.'

She stared at him. 'But—but then, everyone would——'

'Everyone would know that you belong to me. Yes. That's right.' Conor smiled. 'But you've already assured me, there's no risk of you losing our wager.'

She stared at him. 'And what do I get, if I win?'

He smiled. 'Anything your heart wishes, *querida*,' he said, and before she could answer, he tucked her hand into the crook of his arm and walked her into the heart of the fiesta.

The mayor's daughter was a pretty little girl with a tumble of dark curls and a shy smile. She greeted Conor solemnly, but once she'd opened the small, gift-wrapped box he took from his pocket, she shrieked with delight, threw her arms around his neck, and kissed him.

'A teddy bear pin,' Arden said with a little smile as she and Conor melted into the crowd. 'How did you know that would be the perfect gift for her?'

He shrugged. 'She's adored teddy bears ever since she read *Winnie-the-Pooh*.'

'Ah.' Arden linked her arm through his.

Conor's brows lifted. 'And what does that "ah" mean, *señorita*?'

'It means,' she said archly, 'that you're not quite the stubborn, macho fool I thought you were.'

'My God,' he said, 'the woman gave me a compliment.' He stopped dead and tapped a man brushing past them on the shoulder. '*Amigo*,' he said, '*mi amor* just gave me a compliment! Can you believe it?'

The stranger laughed as Arden ducked her head against Conor's shoulder.

'You're awful,' she whispered, but the two simple, wonderful words kept repeating inside her head. My love, he'd said, my love...

'What will it be?' She glanced up. They were standing at a charcoal brazier topped with at least half a dozen

kinds of foods she'd never seen before, all of which were
sending out aromas that made her mouth water. 'Do we
begin with *empanadas*? Or with *gallos*?' Conor clucked
his tongue. 'Or those *puposas*. They look terrific. What
do you think?'

Arden smiled. 'I think I've spent too much time eating
safe *gringo* foods since I've been in Costa Rica. You
decide and surprise me.'

Conor smiled back at her. 'With pleasure, *querida*.'

In the end, he chose one of each, and they shared the
meat and raisin turnover, the stuffed tortilla, and the
fried corn and cheese cake to the last crumb.

'Good?' Conor said.

Arden grinned. 'Better than good. What's next?'

Glasses of *tamarindo* were next, a drink made from
the fruit of the tamarind tree that was tart and delicious,
and then there were more treats to sample, along with
bottles of local beer. The hours slipped by quickly as
they moved through the happy crowd and blended with
it. Conor stopped at a silversmith's stand and bought
Arden a pair of beautiful hoop earrings that she put on
immediately.

'Pretty?' she asked, turning her head so they caught
the light.

'Beautiful,' Conor said, and the way he said it made
her flush with pleasure.

In early afternoon, a *mariachi* band set up just in front
of the church and began to play. The music was sweetly
primitive and very fast, and when Conor drew Arden
into the circle of dancers that had formed, she laughed
in protest.

'I can't dance to this,' she said, but it turned out she
could, that in the warmth and security of Conor's arms
her feet could fly over the old cobblestones with grace
and speed—and then, suddenly, a roar went up ahead.

'What's that?' Arden said.

Conor smiled and put his arm around her waist. 'The bullfight is starting.'

Her good humour faded. 'I've changed my mind,' she said, hanging back as he began leading her forward. 'Conor, listen. I don't want——'

But it was too late. The crowd was surging around them, laughing good-naturedly, carrying them forward whether she wanted it to happen or not...

...and there it was, the bull ring—only it wasn't a ring at all. It was a wooden-fenced pen, and inside it were a smallish black animal looking sleepy in the late afternoon sun and a couple of young boys grinning impishly and waving red cloths.

'Oh,' Arden said, and Conor laughed and put his arm around her waist.

'Noble,' he whispered in her ear, 'and poetic. And what was that other word you used?'

'All right,' she said, tossing her head, 'so they start with something light and funny. But when the *matador* comes along——'

'Those *are* the *matadors*,' Conor said with a chuckle. 'The boys will wave their capes at *el toro* until either they get tired or he does, and then the rancher who brought him leads him home.' He turned her towards him and smiled. 'The boys will boast of their courage to the girls, and the bull will boast of his courage to the cows, and everyone will be happy.'

Arden smiled. 'Truly?'

'Truly, *querida*. That's the way we fight our bulls in my country.'

She giggled. 'I like it.'

'I thought you would.'

'And I'm sorry I was so silly.'

Conor lay his hand against her cheek and lifted her face to his. 'I'm not,' he murmured. 'Have you forgotten our wager?'

Their eyes met. Heat sizzled deep in her belly, raced along her veins and set fire to her body.

'Conor,' she said shakily, 'Conor——'

'Soon, we will go home, *querida*,' he said, and his arm swept around her in a gesture of possession so complete that it stole her breath away.

Now, the hours began to drag. The *fiesta* was still fun, but Arden could think of nothing but what would happen when they reached El Corazon. She had lost the bet they'd made; she was obliged to spend the entire night in Conor's room.

But why had he made the wager? He knew it would embarrass her.

Unless. Her pulses quickened. Unless it was his way of telling her that he was going to mention the word neither of them had used, the word that implied permanency and a life together. Unless, tonight, he was going to tell her he loved her, that he wanted her not only for now but for the rest of his life...

Yes, she thought, oh, yes, that was it! Of course!

The night sky lit with fireworks. Conor drew her closer into the curve of his arm.

'Isn't it perfect, *querida*?' he asked softly.

Arden closed her eyes.

'Perfect,' she whispered.

Thank you, God, she thought, and the fireworks were still there, exploding on her closed lids in exquisite bursts of scarlet.

It was very late when they reached El Corazon. The house lay wreathed in silence, the servants were all gone to their rooms for the night.

Conor opened the door and they stepped quietly inside. He kissed her, put his arm around her waist, and slowly, they climbed the steps to the second floor. At the landing, he paused and turned Arden towards him.

'I've been thinking about our wager,' he said softly.

Her smile was tremulous. 'Yes,' she whispered, 'so have I.'

He smiled back at her and stroked his hand lightly against her flushed cheek.

'I'll understand if you don't want to keep it, sweetheart.'

Arden smiled, loving him all the more for that simple show of understanding.

'Do you want me to keep it?' she asked.

He took her in his arms and kissed her until she was breathless.

'What do you think?' he murmured, pressing his mouth to her hair.

A sigh whispered from her lips. 'I think I want you to take me to your room,' she said softly.

Conor drew back and cupped her shoulders in his hands. He smiled into her eyes, kissed her again, and then lifted her into his arms.

She clasped her arms around his neck and buried her face against his neck while he carried her down the hall to his room. The door snicked shut after them, and he lowered her slowly to the floor. Velvety darkness closed around them.

'How I want you,' Conor whispered. He stroked his fingers lightly over her face and she shut her eyes, hearing only the thudding beat of her heart and the whisper of his breath. '*Mi amor*,' he said thickly, and his hands moved down her throat and across her breasts, his thumbs sweeping in tight arcs over her nipples.

She said his name, her voice broken and husky with desire, and he unbuttoned her blouse and let it fall away from her, unclasped her bra and let it follow the blouse. He kissed her deeply, almost violently, bending her back over his arm, and his hand swept over her body, branding her with flame.

She trembled as he dropped to his knees before her. 'Arden,' he sighed, his breath warm against her belly. She clutched his shoulders for support as he stripped away her skirt, her panties; her knees buckled when he clasped her hips and drew her towards him and when he put his mouth on her, she cried out his name.

'So sweet,' he whispered, tasting her. 'So sweet and fresh, like a flower.'

He rose and pulled off his clothing, and then he took her in his arms again and carried her to the bed. There was a wildness in him tonight, she could feel it in the hard tension of his muscled shoulders, in the sharpness of his teeth as he nipped at her throat.

'Arden,' he said, and he clasped her wrists and drew her hands high over her head. '*Mi amor*,' he whispered, and he entered her, slowly, exquisitely, so that she could feel the power of him filling her inch by inch.

She cried out his name, twisted her hands free, and dug them into his hair, drawing him down to her with a ferocity that matched the rapidly increasing thrusts of his body. She arched up from the bed, locked her legs around his hips, pleading wordlessly for him to bury himself deep within her.

I love you, she thought. She gave a little sob and pressed her lips to his throat, arched as if in pain above her. Oh, Conor, she thought, how I love you!

'*Querida*,' he whispered. He bent to her, caught her mouth with his and kissed her, his tongue moving against hers like silk. He tasted of heat and of the night, of the commingled passion of their straining bodies.

'Look at me, Arden,' he said, in a voice that pleaded as much as it commanded. She did as he'd asked, opening her eyes and focusing on him as he rose above her in the moment that preceded his final possession. 'Yes, like that. Like that...'

He groaned, thrust deep, and Arden cried out, her call a keening note of promise and release that soared upwards into the darkness.

CHAPTER ELEVEN

ARDEN slept dreamlessly, secure in the curve of Conor's arm, her cheek pressed to his shoulder. Just before dawn she stirred. Her hand crept across his chest and she clung more tightly to him in her sleep, her subconscious mind already anticipating—and lamenting—his imminent departure.

But Conor only drew her closer.

'I'm right here, *querida*,' he murmured, pressing a light kiss against her temple.

'Mmm.' She sighed, burrowed against his warmth, and kissed his throat. 'It's almost sunrise,' she whispered sleepily.

He smiled. 'That's wonderful news.' He rolled towards her, settled her firmly against him, and yawned. 'Now, go back to sleep.'

Arden started to shake her head, to remind him that the household would be awakening soon and it was time for him to leave her...

And then she remembered.

She'd lost their wager. Conor wasn't in her bed; she was in his, and she'd promised to stay the entire night.

She thought of Inez, who would surely see them come down the stairs together, of the maid who would see her untouched bed and know it hadn't been slept in, and she stirred uneasily.

'Conor,' she whispered, 'I know we made a bet, but——'

'We did.' He kissed her mouth gently. 'And you lost.'

Arden sighed. 'I know I did,' she said slowly, 'but——'

'*Querida*.' He rose on his elbow and gazed down at her, his face shadowy and mysterious in the pale grey light of early morning. 'I promised we would talk, and we will, at breakfast. Then, I think, you'll feel better about spending the night in my bed.'

She snuggled closer to him and smiled as she stroked the dark hair back from his brow. 'Are you going to offer me another wager I'm certain to lose?'

'Neither of us will lose this time,' Conor said. He cupped her breast, then slid his hand possessively to her hip. 'Unless you think spending the rest of your life here, in my arms, is a penalty.'

Her heart felt as if it were turning over. She'd been right, then. He'd fallen in love with her and he was going to ask her to marry him.

'We could talk now,' she said softly.

'No. Not now. This isn't a time for talking.' Conor's voice roughened as he moved over her. 'We have much better things to do than talk. Isn't that right, *mi amor*?'

Arden caught her breath. 'Yes,' she said, 'oh, yes...'

And then the hurricane of their passion engulfed her, and she gave herself up to it.

When she awoke again, sunlight was streaming into the room and she was alone. The smile that had been blooming on her lips faded. She had dreamed of greeting the morning in Conor's arms, dreamed of kissing him awake.

Her glance shifted to the bedside clock and she shot upright against the pillows. Was it really that late? No wonder Conor was gone. You didn't keep late hours on a ranch, she'd learned that much during the time she'd lived at the *finca*.

And today he'd want to finish his chores quickly, she thought, so he could propose to her at breakfast...

Her smile faded. And so he could be ready to greet Linda, when she arrived this afternoon.

Arden sighed, pushed back the blanket, and got to her feet. In her happiness, she'd almost forgotten about that. Well, it was probably for the best. If there were going to be a confrontation, they might as well get it out of the way. Conor would know how to soothe the girl and make her understand that Arden represented no threat.

She sighed again as she stepped into the shower. Linda would never be her best friend, but surely they could work out some sort of co-operation—especially once Linda knew that she was going to sign over El Corazon to the man who should have been its rightful owner.

The thought brought a smile to her lips. What would Conor say, when she told him she was going to give him the *finca*? She could hardly wait to see the look on his face.

'Conor,' she'd say, before he had the chance to ask her to become his wife, 'I love you with all my heart, and I want you to have El Corazon. It could never belong to anyone but you.'

Just as she could never belong to anyone but him, she thought as she wrapped herself in an oversized towel. A pink flush rose on her skin as she glimpsed herself in the mirrored wall opposite. The long, loving night in Conor's arms had left its mark on her. Her mouth was pink and swollen; her eyes were luminous and soft with pleasure. There was a light bruise on her throat from his teeth and her colour darkened as she thought that she had probably left the same marks of passion on him.

No, she thought, and her heart lifted, no, not just passion. She had given Conor all the love she possessed, and he had given her his in return. She closed her eyes, thinking of how he had caressed her, of how he had whispered to her, called her his love. *Mi amor*, she thought, and she smiled; *mi amor* . . .

It was amazing, how they'd misjudged each other. She had thought him the enemy, but now she knew he was a kind, caring man—and he loved her.

It would have been wonderful if he'd said so, during the night. But she understood his reticence. Men were like that, she supposed; they found it easier to show their feelings than to talk about them—and Conor had surely shown his. She raised her hand to her mouth, where she could almost still feel the heat of his kisses, and then she draped the towel over the rack and hurried into the bedroom.

The things she'd worn to the fiesta were dumped on a chair near the window, crumpled like the petals of an old bouquet. Conor must have scooped the discarded clothing from the floor. A little tremor of pleasure raced through her as she remembered the way he'd undressed her, leaving behind a trail of garments that had wound from the bedroom door to the bed.

She picked up her blouse and skirt and shook them out, but they were both wrinkled beyond repair. Well, there was no choice but to wear them while she went to her own room for a change of clothes.

What was that? The blouse and skirt slipped from her hand and she moved to the dresser, where a white slip of paper with her name scrawled across it stood propped atop a neatly folded pair of faded jeans and a navy T-shirt.

Arden took the note and opened it.

Good morning, querida,
I was going to go to your room and get you some-

thing of your own to put on, but then I decided I'd much rather see you wearing my things. When you're ready, come down to the terrace and join me. We have much to discuss.

Arden shut her eyes. How right he was, she thought, and she brought the note to her lips.

'I love you, Conor,' she whispered.

Quickly, she pulled on the jeans and cotton shirt and ran her fingers through her hair. Then, barefoot, she made her way down the stairs.

The house was quiet, as it always was at this hour of the day. Arden knew the pattern by now. Inez spent her mornings in the kitchen, preparing for lunch and dinner, overseeing the maids who giggled softly to each other as they pared vegetables or polished silver.

Ordinarily, Conor would be riding the *finca*, checking on the cattle and the horses and the coffee shrubs. Or perhaps he'd be in the library, frowning over the ledgers—but not today.

Arden smiled as she padded quietly down the hall. Today, he'd be waiting for her, waiting to tell her that he wanted her for the rest of his life, that he . . .

'. . . ridiculous! Absolutely ridiculous, Conor! How could you let this happen?'

The voice was coming from the library, snaking out the half-opened door like a cold draught. Arden stumbled to a halt, her smile gone. No, she thought unhappily, oh, no, please, don't let it be Linda. Not yet. She wasn't due until hours from now.

'Who would believe such a thing, Conor? Surely, not your attorneys!'

Arden sank back against the wall. It was Linda, all right. There was no mistaking that husky voice, even though anger had honed it to a sharp edge.

'You told me—*assured* me—that this codicil is not worth the paper it's written on!'

Arden blew out her breath. Linda was talking about the will.

'Linda.' Conor spoke with quiet patience. 'Listen to me.'

'No,' the girl said angrily. 'Why should I? I listened and listened, and where did it lead me?'

'Linda, *mi amor*, please. Calm down and try and understand.'

Mi amor. Arden swallowed drily. My love. That was what he called her, not Linda . . .

She gave herself a little shake. What nonsense! It was like any other term of endearment. You could call your sister your love, or your cousin—or your lover. The special meaning came from the way you said the words, not from the words themselves.

'I tell you, I *did* listen,' Linda said angrily. 'I listened when you told me Felix would come to care for me in good time, but he never did. I listened when you said I would never have to worry——'

'And you won't,' Conor said. 'Have I ever let you down? Have I?'

Arden bit down on her lip. It was wrong to stand here and listen to this. Linda was upset about things that were private, family matters she didn't yet understand.

But what should she do? Should she walk the few steps to the library door or clear her throat loudly, let Conor and Linda know she'd overheard them? Should she tiptoe back the way she'd come, go to her room and wait for Conor to come looking for her?

'She has no right to El Corazon, Conor. None whatsoever! You know it as well as I do.'

Arden heard what had to be the sound of Conor's expelled breath. 'Of course I know it,' he said.

Her hand flew to her mouth. She hadn't been foolish enough to think that Conor would have suddenly decided he was happy that Felix had left the ranch to her, not even now that they'd fallen in love, but there'd been such anger in his words, such bitterness...

Linda's heels tapped sharply against the floor and Arden shut her eyes, imagining the brunette stalking towards Conor.

'Then do something about it.'

'I can't,' Conor's voice was flat and without expression.

'What do you mean, you can't? I knew better than to ever dream Felix would leave El Corazon to me, but surely—*surely*—we both expected he would leave it to you! Instead, he scribbles a meaningless note and leaves your rightful inheritance to this—this woman who you admit is little more than a tramp?'

Arden fell back against the wall, her knuckle caught between her teeth. No, she thought, no, this couldn't be happening. Linda was upset, and Conor was trying to soothe her. Any second now, he'd tell his cousin to shut her mouth, to be careful what she said about the woman he loved.

'You're wrong,' Conor said sharply, and Arden almost sobbed with relief.

'I am not wrong! He was senile!'

'Come on, Linda, we both know he was as sharp as a tack.'

'Our attorneys will prove otherwise.'

'Our attorneys will grow rich in the attempt.' Conor's footsteps stomped across the hardwood floor. 'They're the only ones who profit in cases such as this.'

Arden's eyes widened. That was what Conor had said before, when he'd told her how he'd tricked Felix into giving up the cloud forest. It had seemed so clever then, his ability to get something from someone who didn't want to give it.

No. No, that couldn't be where this conversation was heading... An iron fist formed in her stomach.

'I see,' Linda said icily. 'So, this woman forces herself into our lives, convinces Felix that she cares for him more than we do——'

'She probably did,' Conor said with a little laugh. 'But then, she didn't know him as well as we did.'

'The point is, she stole El Corazon out from under your nose. *Por Dios*, Conor, what will become of me?'

Conor sighed. 'I'll take care of you, *querida*. I always have, and I always will.'

'And this woman will walk off with the *finca*?'

'Her name is Arden.'

'Arden.' Linda fairly spat the name. 'A *gringa* name! It makes me ill even to say it!'

'Perhaps. But you'd better get used to saying it.'

'Why should I? You've just told me, you're not going to fight her in court, as you should.'

'No, I'm not.' Conor paused. 'I'm going to marry her, instead.'

'Marry her? This—this fortune hunter? Conor, *mi amor*, have you lost your mind?'

Conor laughed. 'On the contrary. I've only just found it.'

'Please, tell me this is a bad joke! I know you want El Corazon, but surely not so badly that you would tie yourself to this—this scheming *gringa*!'

'Linda.' Conor's voice was gentle. 'Sit down and I'll explain.'

'You don't have to explain. I'm not an idiot. You'll marry her and gain the *finca*.'

'That's how it will work out, yes.'

'No! No, I don't believe you! You can't want anything that much.'

'But I do,' Conor said, so softly that Arden could barely hear him. 'I do, Linda. Believe me, you can't imagine how much!'

Arden clamped her hand over her mouth and spun away from the wall. She could hear Conor's voice droning on and on, but the words were unintelligible. Good, she thought with a choked sob, because she didn't want to hear any more. God, she *couldn't* hear any more, not if she wanted to stay strong enough to pack her things and get out of this house.

She flew up the stairs, her bare feet soundless against the carpeted steps, and raced down the hall to her room. Once inside, she shut the door after her, locked it, and sank back against it.

Tears filled her eyes, overflowed and spilled down her cheeks. She wanted to hurl herself on the bed, weep and weep until there was nothing left inside her heart but dust.

But there was no time for that. Not now.

She raised her arm, wiped her streaming eyes, then stopped and glared at her damp sleeve. This was Conor's shirt, not hers—and these were his jeans she was wearing.

A shudder went through her. It was obscene, feeling his clothing against her skin. Quickly, she ripped the things from her body and kicked them into the corner. Naked, she pulled clothing blindly from the dresser, underwear and a shirt and cotton trousers...

And then she stopped. She would leave El Corazon as she had come to it, she thought, not sneaking out the door with her face tear-streaked and her hair hanging down her back, but with what little dignity she could manage. She yanked open the closet door, took a steadying breath, and reached for a hanger.

A short while later, dressed in a beige silk blouse, white linen suit, and matching pumps, Arden tossed the last of her clothing into her suitcase and snapped it closed. She stood erect, smoothed down her skirt with a trembling hand. All that remained now was to confront Conor, tell him she knew what he'd been up to, tell him...

Breath puffed from her lungs. Tell him what? she thought, and the anger that had protected her the last few minutes began to crumple. Tell him that she'd been as stupid as any of those silly girls she'd grown up with, that she'd let herself fall in love with a no-good aristocrat from the top of the Hill? Tell him she'd gone against all her beliefs, that she'd given him her heart and her soul, that she'd never feel whole or clean again?

No. No, she couldn't let him see her this way, she'd fall apart if she had to face him, she'd——

'Arden?'

Her heart leapt into her throat. Conor was just outside.

'Arden?' The knob rattled and her gaze flew to the door, as if she expected it to give way at any moment. 'Arden, are you in there?'

She spun in a quick circle, staring around the room as if by some miracle an opening might suddenly appear in one of the walls.

'Arden?' Conor's voice, and the rap of his fist, had grown more insistent. '*Mi amor*, are you all right?'

Mi amor, she thought, *mi amor*...

Head high, she strode across the room, undid the lock, and flung the door open. Conor gave her a smile, one that was so sincere it would have fooled anybody. Anybody but her, she thought, and a fist seemed to clamp around her heart.

'There you are. I was worried, sweetheart. You weren't in my room, and when I tried your door...' He broke off, frowning. 'Why are you dressed like that?'

You can do this, Arden told herself, you *must* do this. She smiled politely. 'Like what?'

'I thought we'd spend the day riding into the hills. You wanted to see the coffee fields, and——'

'Oh, that's OK. I'll see them, eventually, won't I?'

Conor's smile was puzzled. 'Well, sure. I mean, if you'd rather ride another day...tomorrow, maybe, or——'

'Not tomorrow,' Arden said, forcing a little laugh. She turned and walked to the mirror, looked into it, and adjusted her collar. 'I doubt if I'll see those fields, or any other part of El Corazon, for several more months.'

Behind her, in the mirror, she could see Conor's reflection, see his mouth thin. Her heart began to beat more rapidly as he walked slowly towards her.

'Arden. What's going on here?'

'What do you mean?'

His hands fell on her shoulders and he swung her towards him. 'Don't play games,' he said tightly. The muscle in his cheek clenched. 'Tell me what this is all about.'

'Hey,' she said with a little smile, 'ease up, will you? Don't try and blame this on me! I kept saying I had to talk to you, but——'

'And I agreed. We have a lot of talking to do.' His hands tightened on her shoulders. 'Serious talking. And now, I come up here and I find you dressed like this, with your suitcase on the bed——'

'Well, it's not my fault, Conor. If you'd just given me a chance yesterday, you'd understand.'

A tight smile twitched across his mouth. 'I'm listening.'

Arden looked into his eyes. They weren't green, not now. They were black as ebony, and cold in a way that terrified her.

And yet, what was there to be afraid of? Nothing Conor Martinez could do or say would ever hurt her half as much as what he'd already done. She wanted to tell him that, to lash out at him and hurt him, but it was hard to hurt somebody without a heart. You could only do it by pretending you didn't have one, either.

'Well?' His fingers bit into her flesh.

Arden took a deep, deep breath. 'I'm going.'

An eternity seemed to drag by before he answered. 'Going? Going where?'

'Come on, Conor, don't let's drag this out.' She twisted away from him and walked to the bed, where her suitcase lay waiting. 'This has been very pleasant, but——'

'Pleasant?' She closed her eyes, then blinked them open, as she heard him cross the room towards her. 'Pleasant?' he said again, his voice a snarl as he spun her to face him.

The rage flaming in his eyes was enough to make her tremble, but she couldn't do that. She couldn't show any weakness, not now, not ever, not to this man. Arden reached deep inside herself and drew on the well of strength that had always seen her through.

'I know you thought I'd stay here until the will was through probate,' she said calmly. 'Well, I did, too, for a while, but——'

'To hell with the will!'

'—but with the rainy season coming and all——'

'Are you crazy? What does the rainy season have to do with us?'

'Us?' Arden widened her eyes. 'Us? What's that supposed to mean?'

'You know what it means,' he said through his teeth. 'I'm in love with you, Arden, and you're in love with me!'

'Love!' She laughed. 'Oh, Conor, I'm flattered, but——'

She cried out as he grasped her arm and twisted it behind her. Fear put a metallic taste into her mouth; it made her heart bang against her ribs, but she forced herself to show none of it as she looked into his face.

'Don't,' she said softly. 'You've lost El Corazon, Conor. You wouldn't want to face an assault charge, too.'

He gave her a look that was so filled with hate and loathing that she felt the coldness of it stab into her soul. His hand closed on her throat; she gave a little gasp as he tilted her head back and leaned towards her.

'I was right about you all along,' he said softly. 'You're a cold-blooded, grasping bitch!'

'What's the matter, Conor? Did you really think I'd let you seduce me into giving away what's mine?'

'Bitch,' he whispered again, his fingers tightening on her throat.

'It's going to be hard to explain thumb prints on my neck to a judge, Señor Martinez.'

'You got exactly what you wanted, didn't you?' he growled.

Arden felt the sharp bite of tears behind her eyes.

'I told you,' she said, 'women like me get exactly what they deserve.'

There was a long silence, and then Conor's lips curled back from his teeth in a smile she knew she would never forget.

'Remember what I told you about the legal juggernaut?' He stepped closer to her, drew her towards him, until his mouth was a whisper from hers. 'Take my advice, sweetheart. Look for someplace to hide, because you're about to get rolled over.' His hand fell from her throat and he strode to the door. 'I'd ask Pablo to drive you to the airport, but you're liable to corrupt him. Take the Bronco and leave it there. I'll have it picked up and disinfected after you're gone.'

The door opened, then slammed shut, and Arden was alone.

CHAPTER TWELVE

ARDEN eased her keys from her pocket, unlocked the door to her Manhattan apartment, and edged it open with her hip. She stepped inside, bumped the door shut, and dropped the dresses she'd picked up at the dry cleaners on a chair. Then she made her way to the kitchen, dumped her bag and the grocery sack on the countertop, and flicked on the overhead fluorescent light.

Light bathed the little room, chasing away the unexpected gloom of the midsummer evening, but then this hadn't been anything like a usual summer so far, Arden thought as she took a quart of milk, a small loaf of bread and two oranges from the bag. She'd returned from Costa Rica almost five months ago to what should have been a gentle New York spring. Instead, a chill April had given way to a wet May, which had been followed by record-breaking heat in June. Now, with August hard on the heels of an even hotter July, the skies had all but ripped open, sending down torrents of rain that had eventually thinned to an on again, off again drizzle.

City dwellers had been grateful at first.

'It's cooling things off, thank heavens,' Irene, the secretary in the office down the hall at work had said when the rain began.

But as umbrella sales soared, spirits began to sag.

'Awful stuff, this weather,' Irene had said glumly this morning at coffee-break time. 'But just imagine if you'd stayed in Costa Rica! It's the rainy season there, isn't it? You'd have shrivelled up like a prune by now!'

Arden had laughed politely and said yes, she probably would have, and then she'd discreetly steered the conversation elsewhere, just as she'd done every time someone mentioned Costa Rica since she'd returned home. The amazing thing was that no one had so much as suggested she'd been trying to avoid the topic. People had their own agendas, even the most astute. So long as you nodded in the right places and offered an occasional 'yes' or 'uh huh' to the conversation, you really didn't have to say much of anything. The personnel director who'd hired her for this new job had said, Oh, Costa Rica, wasn't that exciting? And then she'd launched into a five-minute description of the two weeks she'd spent in Venezuela, years before, at the end of which she'd smiled, extended her hand, and said Arden was hired.

Even Arden's mother hadn't asked many questions.

'You're back sooner than you thought you'd be, aren't you?' Evelyn had said, and Arden—who'd had her mail forwarded to El Corazon from San José but had never told her mother the ugly story of how she'd lost one job and taken on another—had shrugged and mumbled something about the job being finished quicker than anticipated.

'And how was Costa Rica?' Evelyn had asked, and before Arden could offer more than a cautious, 'OK,' her mother had asked if she'd had the chance to see any of the beautiful mansions she'd heard existed in some parts of Central America. Arden had hesitated, then said yes, she had, and she'd described El Corazon to an enthralled Evelyn until the older woman had interrupted.

'How magnificent,' she'd sighed. 'But who owns it?'

Arden had stared at her mother. I do, she'd thought with a sudden start—but before she could answer, an unbidden image of Conor had risen up before her as clearly as if he were in the room with them, Conor, tall and handsome and dangerously masculine. To her horror, her throat had constricted and she'd dragged a handkerchief from her pocket and pressed it to her mouth.

'Sorry,' she'd said, clearing her throat briskly. 'I must have picked up a bug.'

Evelyn had tut-tutted in sympathy. 'Who knows what's floating around in the jungle?' she'd said, and Arden had skilfully led the discussion elsewhere, before her mother could bring it back to dangerous waters.

Arden folded the empty grocery sack neatly, put it away in the broom cupboard, and turned to the refrigerator. What would tonight's gourmet treat be? she thought wryly as she peered into the freezer. Chicken Alfredo? *Filet* of sole? *Boeuf aux champignons*? She made a face and plucked out a package at random.

'Garden lasagna,' she read aloud as she tore off the paper covering, then set the plastic dish in the microwave oven.

Not that it mattered, she thought, unzipping her dress as she made her way down the hall to the bedroom. Frozen dinners all tasted exactly the same, no matter what the label promised. But they were quick and required no planning, something she wasn't too good at lately. Perhaps when the weekend came round, she'd take the time to cook for herself...

And then again, she thought, sighing as she stepped from her dress and kicked off her shoes, perhaps she wouldn't. It seemed an awful lot of trouble to go through for one person, shopping for meat and vegetables and such, measuring and tasting and timing, when in truth it didn't much matter if she sat down to the finest meal cooked by a cordon bleu chef or to the least distinguishable blob to come off a food packager's assembly line.

Everything tasted like straw, ever since she'd come back from Costa Rica.

Arden sighed again as slipped on a pair of cotton trousers and an oversized washed silk T-shirt. The simple truth was that she couldn't seem to get excited about anything since she'd come home, not even about her new job, which was crazy because it was really a terrific job, much better paying than the last, with lots more responsibilities and opportunities for advancement.

'It's the weather,' she mumbled aloud as she took the plastic dish from the microwave oven. Of course it was. The heat, the rain—it was enough to make anybody feel depressed.

She tore back the top seal and sniffed at the greyish stuff inside the dish, grimacing with distaste before setting the dish on the table and taking a fork and napkin from the drawer. She sat down, put the napkin in her lap, and stabbed at the mess.

What did she mean, depressed? She wasn't 'depressed'. Why should she be? she thought, holding her breath as she chewed a mouthful of tonight's dinnertime treat and then swallowed it down. She had a great new job, her apartment—paid for all the months she'd been gone by McCann, Flint, Emerson—seemed none the worse for having stood empty, and autumn would be coming on soon, which meant the city would roll into high gear and opera, ballet, the symphony orchestra and new Broadway productions would offer themselves up like a smorgasbord of cultural delights. The man Irene worked for, a nice enough sort whose mid-western accent and easy manner confirmed Irene's whispered tale of his having worked his way up from office boy, had been suggesting lately that it would be nice to attend some of those events together.

'You ought to take the guy up on it,' Irene kept saying. 'He's really awfully nice.'

And he was, Arden thought, putting down her fork and shoving the horrible little plastic dish away. But she wasn't any more interested in getting involved with anybody now than she'd been before she'd gone to Costa Rica, not even someone who was unpretentious and self-made, who tried very hard to make her smile—who was tall and dark-haired and, at a distance, a very great distance, might almost be mistaken for Conor. But he wasn't Conor, he never would be; he hadn't Conor's charm not his swift temper, he couldn't make her heart stop with just a smile or a softly whispered word...

'Damn!'

Arden shot up from the table, grabbed the frozen dinner, and plopped it into the garbage bin. What was the matter with her tonight? Charm? Conor had charm, all right, the sort conmen had relied upon for years. As for his soft whispers, she thought grimly, they'd been about as substantial as cobwebs.

Not that she cared. By now, she knew that she'd never loved him at all. What she'd been was dazzled—by his looks, by his charlatan's practised charm—no, she thought as she strode into the living-room and sank down at the old *secretaire* she'd salvaged from the flea market on Third Avenue, no, she'd never cared one little bit for Conor Martinez. If she'd just kept to the opinion she'd had of him right from the start, she'd have saved herself lots of time and tears.

At least, it would be over soon. Arden's jaw firmed as she pulled open the top drawer of the *secretaire* and withdrew an envelope stuffed with papers. She pulled them out, spread them across the desktop, and riffled through them. Felix's will had passed through probate, and El Corazon was now officially hers. The letter of formal notification had arrived two weeks ago, and now she could shut the door on this part of her life.

Arden smoothed the letter open and read it for perhaps the tenth time.

'Dear Miss Miller: I am pleased to inform you that...'

Her eyes skimmed the page. Yes, it was true. The *finca* belonged to her now. Conor had lost his bid for it—if you could call the one effort he'd made at getting the codicil invalidated a 'bid'. A grim smile touched Arden's lips. Conor had threatened she'd be run over by a legal juggernaut but, in the end, he'd backed off.

His lawyers had notified hers that he was going to fight the will, hers had fired back a reply warning that she was prepared to dig in her heels and fight—and, after a lengthy silence, Conor had surrendered.

'My letter of intent convinced his legal staff of the strength of our case,' Arden's lawyer had wired proudly.

Arden had let him think what he liked, but she'd known the truth, that it was Conor's unremitting practicality that had won out over his hatred of her.

'Attorneys are the only people who profit in cases like this,' he'd said.

And that, plain and simple, was why El Corazon was hers now, without a prolonged legal battle. She'd been right about Conor all along. He hadn't wanted the *finca* so much as he'd wanted to avenge his father. And as for her—in the end, he hadn't even hated her enough to squander money fighting her. She'd been a disturbance in his life, nothing more, nothing less. By now, he'd probably forgotten all about her, forgotten those nights she'd spent in his arms, forgotten all the things she would never forget...

Arden's breath hissed between her teeth.

'Stop it,' she said, her voice angry and sharp in the silence. 'You're behaving like a fool!'

The ranch was hers now, hers and no one else's, and—and . . .

And she didn't want it. Winning El Corazon had seemed a victory, but now she saw it for what it was, for what it always would be: a bittersweet reminder of pain and sorrow, an open wound that would never heal so long as she was mistress of El Corazon. But what choice did she have? She could sell it, of course, but the thought of knowing that someone other than Conor was riding that land was unsettling. It was crazy, of course, because she hated Conor with every breath she took, but that was the way she——

'Wait a minute,' she whispered. A little smile began curving across her lips. Conor had threatened Felix with some organisation when the old man had wanted to sell the cloud forest. What was it called? Friends of the Land? The Forest Conservers?

'Friends of the Forest,' she said delightedly, and her smile became a grin.

By this time next week, she'd be free of El Corazon and all it stood for, forever.

But it took longer than that even to set the wheels in motion.

'I want to give El Corazon to Friends of the Forest,' she told her attorney when she phoned him the next day.

'What?' he said. 'We have a poor connection, *señorita*. I thought, for a moment, you said you wanted to give El Corazon to——'

'That's exactly what I said. Contact them, please, and draw up the necessary papers.'

It was obvious he thought she'd lost her *gringa* mind. 'You must think about this,' he kept saying through phone call after phone call, until Arden called the organisation herself and asked them if they'd be interested in being gifted with a hundred thousand plus acres of land in Costa Rica.

Two months later, everything was in place. The phone lines had hummed between San José and New York, she had signed what seemed hundreds of papers, and now all that remained was the one final paper, the deed that would give El Corazon to the organisation for all time to come.

The organisation's secretary telephoned Arden at work late one Friday afternoon.

'Our representative is in New York, Miss Miller,' he said. 'We hoped we could arrange a Press conference for tomorrow.'

'No Press conference,' she said firmly. 'I thought I'd explained, I want this all done very quietly.'

There was a brief pause. 'Are you sure? This is quite a large gift, after all, and we should like to acknowledge your kindness in some way.'

'Acknowledge it by keeping the *finca* as it is,' she said. She closed her eyes, envisaging the horses grazing the dark green pastures, the rolling hills, and suddenly she saw Conor in her mind's eye, Conor, carrying her into the shadowy coolness of a forest clearing. Her throat closed. 'Just—just live up to your agreement,' she said in a small, choked whisper. 'Let El Corazon live on forever as it was, as it might have been . . .'

'As it will always be,' a soft, deep voice said.

Arden's head shot up and there was Conor, standing in the doorway of her office, wearing a dark suit, a white shirt and red silk tie, looking as urbane and sophisticated as the day she'd first learned his true identity. But she could sense the elemental man lurking just beneath the civilised veneer, the power and passion that marked him as the Master of El Corazon.

The phone fell from her hand and clattered to the desk.

'Conor?' she breathed.

He smiled as he walked towards her. 'Hello, Arden.'

She put her hands in her lap and laced the fingers together. 'What—what are you doing here?'

'You've lost weight,' he said quietly, his gaze flickering over her.

Get hold of yourself, Arden told herself fiercely.

'Well,' she said with a quick little smile, 'you know what they say. You can never be too rich or too thin.'

'But you can be, *querida*. You can be so rich you see money as power, as a whip you can use to beat people into submission.' The muscle in his cheek knotted and unknotted. 'Felix was a master of it.'

'Is that why you came here? To talk about your uncle?'

He stopped beside her desk, hung up the phone, then ran his hand lightly along her cheek. She caught her breath, fighting against the sudden, dizzying desire to press her mouth to his hand. 'There are hollows here, beneath your cheekbones,' he said softly. 'Why have you lost so much weight, *querida*?'

Her laughter was quick and brittle. 'I told you, there's no such thing as being too rich or too thin. Now that I'm rich——'

'You are not rich, *querida*.' His hand slid down her throat, whispered across her breast and paused above her racing heart. 'Here, where it matters, you are as poor as I am.'

Arden struck his hand away. 'I don't know what you're talking about,' she said sharply. 'Anyway, I'm hardly "poor" any more—or have you forgotten that I won the fight for El Corazon?'

'What fight? I didn't oppose you.'

'You were afraid of your own prophecy coming true.'

His brow furrowed. 'Prophecy?'

'You knew you'd lose, Conor, and so you decided not to waste money on a bunch of low-life lawyers.'

'You're sure of that,' he said with a little smile.

'The only thing I'm not sure of is why you've come here.'

He smiled again as he reached for her hand and drew her to her feet. 'You know why.'

'No,' she insisted, 'I don't, but...'

But what? He was looking at her as he had the day they'd gone to the fiesta, when he'd said he wanted to tell her something important and she, poor fool that she'd been, had thought he'd wanted to tell her he'd fallen in love with her. *Oh, God, oh, God, let me stop remembering...*

Arden lifted her chin. 'Are you trying to get me fired? Reception didn't announce you—I don't suppose you bothered with a pass. The company has rules against personal visitors.'

'A visitor? Is that all I am, *mi amor*?'

Arden's heart skipped a beat. 'Don't—don't call me that!' she said unsteadily.

'Why?' He brought her hand to his mouth and kissed the palm. 'In my heart, you are *mi amor*. You always will be.'

'Linda,' she said, the words tumbling uncontrolled from her lips in a fierce whisper. 'Linda is your love, she's...'

She stared at him, horrified. What was she saying? What was she doing? She was making a fool of herself in front of this—this arrogant, deceitful, lying, cheating——

And, all at once, she knew why he had come.

'You know about El Corazon,' she said slowly, her eyes on his.

'That you're giving it away? Yes.'

'You're unbelievable!' Arden wrenched her hand free of his. 'Did you really think you could come here and—and sweet-talk me into changing my mind and giving you the *finca* instead?'

'I came here to ask you a question, Arden.' Conor leaned back against her desk, his arms folded over his chest. 'Why did you decide to give away the ranch you so desperately wanted?'

'Me?' Arden laughed bitterly. 'I never wanted El Corazon. You were the one who——' She broke off in confusion, realising she'd said too much. 'It's none of your business,' she said, starting past him, but Conor caught hold of her wrist and stopped her.

'The day you ran away——'

'I never ran away!'

'You ran off, like a frightened child, *querida*.' His mouth twisted. 'And I reacted like a stubborn one and let you go.'

'Listen, Conor, this analysis is fascinating, but——'

'That day, when you left me, you said you'd never wanted me, that it had been the ranch you'd wanted all along.'

'I never said...' He began to smile and she flushed. 'You're twisting everything that went on that day, dammit!'

'Ah, *mi amor*.' He bent his head and brushed his mouth lightly over hers. Arden jerked her head away, but not before her heart had given an agonizing leap. 'We must do something about that wicked tongue of yours,' he whispered softly, cupping her chin in his hand so that she had no choice but to meet his emerald gaze.

'Conor, this won't work. You're trying to—to confuse me, to make me agree to give you the ranch, but——'

'That was part of our trouble, sweetheart.' He smiled and slipped his arms around her. 'I was so positive I knew what you were up to, and you were absolutely certain you understood my every move.'

She stiffened in his embrace. 'I heard everything you and Linda said to each other that day. So if you're going to try and pretend I misunderstood——'

'Yes.' His smile vanished. 'It took months before I let my head do my thinking instead of my heart. When I did, I began to think you must have been in the hallway, listening to Linda.'

'And to you,' she said coldly.

He nodded. 'And to me—and misinterpreting every word.'

'Listen, Conor, you're wasting your time. I told you, I know what you want. You're hoping you can convince me that—that you care for me, so that you can make me sign the ranch over to you, but——'

'Why on earth would I do that,' he asked, gently drawing her unyielding body closer to him, 'when you've already done all the work for me?'

Arden stared at him blankly. 'What are you talking about?'

'I'm talking about all the red tape involved in giving the *finca* to Friends of the Forest, sweetheart.' Conor linked his hands behind her back and grinned. 'Of course, I'd make my lawyers happy, duplicating all those documents, but——'

'Duplicating what documents?'

'Arden, *mi amor*, you've stolen my idea.' He smiled, bent to her, and kissed her. 'And I love you for it.'

'Have you gone crazy, Conor? I don't understand anything you're saying!'

'It's very simple, *querida*. Do you remember the day of the fiesta? I made you sleep with me the entire night.'

'You made a bet you knew I'd lose,' she said, her cheeks flaming.

'Only because I couldn't bear the thought of not holding you in my arms, sweetheart—and because I knew that, the next morning, I would ask you to become my wife.'

'Yes.' Her heart felt like a piece of ice lying cold within her breast. 'I heard you tell that to Linda.'

'Of course I told it to Linda,' he said impatiently. 'I know you think she's a spoiled brat——'

'Hah!'

'Perhaps she is—but she's also an unhappy young woman. Don't turn away from me, *querida*,' he said, clasping her face in his hand. 'Listen with your heart this time, imagine her not as she is now but as a little girl, eager for the love of a father—and having Felix turn away her every childish gesture of affection.'

'So, she turned to you instead,' Arden said coldly.

'Yes, she did.' His hand held her firmly, so she couldn't look away from him. 'And I loved her as she loved me, Arden, as brother and sister. I promised her I would always take care of her, that I would never abandon her.'

'This is all interesting, Conor, but it has nothing to do with me. I'm not going to tumble back into bed with you, I'm not going to give you El Corazon——'

'Dammit,' he said gruffly, 'haven't you heard a word I said? I don't want the ranch.'

'You've always wanted it!'

'Once, perhaps. But you made me see the truth: that I only wanted it to avenge my father.' His hand slipped to the nape of her neck, his fingers burrowing into her hair. 'I realised that, the day of the fiesta.'

'That's easy to say now, Conor, but why didn't you tell me it then?'

'I was going to, at breakfast.' He drew a deep breath. 'I was going to tell you that I loved you with all my heart and ask you to marry me.' He leaned his forehead against hers. 'But I suspected you wouldn't believe me—unless we found a way to deal with El Corazon.'

Arden ran the tip of her tongue across her lips. Her heart was batting against her ribs, her pulse was racing—but why should she believe anything this man said? He was a liar, a fraud, he was everything she despised...

No, no, he wasn't. A little sob rose in her throat and she clamped her lips together to smother it. Who was she kidding? Conor was everything she loved and would always love, and if he had come here to break her heart again...

'You're right,' she said, her eyes fixed to his. 'I wouldn't have believed you.'

Conor nodded. 'Exactly. So I found the perfect solution. I would donate the ranch to the same group I'd threatened Felix with when he'd wanted to sell the cloud forest—Friends of the Forest.'

Arden's eyes widened. 'What?'

'I don't need El Corazon, Arden. What I told you is true: I made more money than my uncle ever did, once I'd figured out that growing bananas and shipping them, along with raising coffee and sugar and cattle on my own *finca* in Venezuela, was a lot more profitable than spending my life in a sulk. In fact, for the last few years, it's been my money that's kept El Corazon from going under. Felix had made some poor decisions and investments.'

'He never told me that,' she said, surprised. 'He only said you'd been interfering...'

Conor sighed. 'I don't think he ever really let himself acknowledge the truth. He was too proud and too stubborn—traits that run in the family, I'm afraid.' He smiled and clasped her face in his hands. 'The day of the fiesta, I knew, without question, that you weren't after money, that you never had been, that you were the kindest, sweetest woman a man could ever be lucky enough to find.'

Tears rose in Arden's eyes. 'But—but I thought... I heard you agree with Linda, that I was a fortune hunter——'

'No!' Conor shook his head angrily. 'No, *querida*, you could never have heard me say such a thing, because I knew it wasn't true. I can't deny that Linda believed those things of you, but I told her that you were the most important thing in my life, that she couldn't begin to understand how much I wanted you.'

A sob broke from Arden's lips. 'Oh, Conor,' she whispered, 'when I heard the things she said—when I thought you were agreeing with her—I wanted to die.'

He lifted her face to him. 'Then you do love me,' he said, triumph shining in his eyes.

She sighed. 'Of course I love you. I thought—I thought you'd used me, I thought...' She shook her head. 'I misjudged you so badly,' she said brokenly. 'All I could think of was—was how you'd hurt me——'

'—and, to protect yourself, you wanted to hurt me in return.' Conor gathered her close in his arms and brought her head to his chest. She closed her eyes and listened to the wonderful, steady beat of his heart.

'I'm sorry, *mi amor*,' he said softly. 'I should never have doubted you. I should have realised you could never be the woman you tried so hard to make me think you were.'

She smiled tremulously, put her arms around his neck, and leaned back in his embrace.

'Will you miss El Corazon, do you think?'

Conor smiled back at her. 'Will you miss New York?'

'How could I, when I'll have you?'

'Exactly, *querida*. It's the same for me.' He kissed her again, deeply and sweetly, and then he pressed his mouth to her temple. 'The organisation will take good care of the *finca*. I think even Felix would be pleased—but I can't help wondering what he'd say if he knew this was the "new beginning" he spoke of.'

Arden framed Conor's face in her hands. 'You know something?' she said, very softly. 'I have the definite feeling he does know—and that he approves.'

Conor smiled. 'My uncle was right, *mi amor*,' he whispered. 'You are, indeed, a very clever *gringa*.'

And then he put his arm around her, and led her out of the office and into the street, where despite the rush of New York traffic, Arden was certain she could smell the sweet, clean breeze that blew across El Corazon.

Coming Next Month

HARLEQUIN PRESENTS®

THE BEST HAS JUST GOTTEN BETTER!

#1929 A MARRIAGE TO REMEMBER Carole Mortimer
Three years ago Adam Carmichael had walked out on Maggi—now he was back! Divorce seemed the only way to get him out of her life for good. But Adam wasn't going to let her go without a fight!

#1930 RED-HOT AND RECKLESS Miranda Lee
(Scandals!)
Ben Sinclair just couldn't put his schoolboy obsession with Amber behind him. She *still* thought she could have anything because she was rich and beautiful. But now Ben had a chance to get even with her at last....

#1931 TIGER, TIGER Robyn Donald
Leo Dacre was determined to find out what had happened to his runaway half brother, but Tansy was just as determined not to tell him! It was a clash of equals...so who would be the winner?

#1932 FLETCHER'S BABY Anne McAllister
Sam Fletcher never ran away from difficult situations, so when Josie revealed that she was expecting his child, marriage seemed the practical solution. And he wasn't going to take no for an answer!

#1933 THE SECRET MOTHER Lee Wilkinson
(Nanny Wanted!)
Caroline had promised herself that one day she would be back for Caitlin. Now, four years later, she's applying for the job of her nanny. Matthew Carran, the interviewer, doesn't *seem* to recognize her. But he has a hidden agenda....

#1934 HUSBAND BY CONTRACT Helen Brooks
(Husbands and Wives)
For Donato Vittoria, marriage was a lifetime commitment. Or so Grace had thought—until she'd discovered his betrayal, and fled. But in Donato's eyes he was still her husband, and he wanted her back in his life—and in his bed!

**Don't miss these Harlequin favorites
by some of our bestselling authors! Act now and
receive a discount by ordering two or more titles!**

HT#25720	A NIGHT TO REMEMBER	$3.50 U.S.	☐
	by Gina Wilkins	$3.99 CAN.	☐
HT#25722	CHANGE OF HEART	$3.50 U.S.	☐
	by Janice Kaiser	$3.99 CAN.	☐
HP#11797	A WOMAN OF PASSION	$3.50 U.S.	☐
	by Anne Mather	$3.99 CAN.	☐
HP#11863	ONE-MAN WOMAN	$3.50 U.S.	☐
	by Carole Mortimer	$3.99 CAN.	☐
HR#03356	BACHELOR'S FAMILY	$2.99 U.S.	☐
	by Jessica Steele	$3.50 CAN.	☐
HR#03441	RUNAWAY HONEYMOON	$3.25 U.S.	☐
	by Ruth Jean Dale	$3.75 CAN.	☐
HS#70715	BAREFOOT IN THE GRASS	$3.99 U.S.	☐
	by Judith Arnold	$4.50 CAN.	☐
HS#70729	ANOTHER MAN'S CHILD	$3.99 U.S.	☐
	by Tara Taylor Quinn	$4.50 CAN.	☐
HI#22361	LUCKY DEVIL	$3.75 U.S.	☐
	by Patricia Rosemoor	$4.25 CAN.	☐
HI#22379	PASSION IN THE FIRST DEGREE	$3.75 U.S.	☐
	by Carla Cassidy	$4.25 CAN.	☐
HAR#16638	LIKE FATHER, LIKE SON	$3.75 U.S.	☐
	by Mollie Molay	$4.25 CAN.	☐
HAR#16663	ADAM'S KISS	$3.75 U.S.	☐
	by Mindy Neff	$4.25 CAN.	☐
HH#28937	GABRIEL'S LADY	$4.99 U.S.	☐
	by Ana Seymour	$5.99 CAN.	☐
HH#28941	GIFT OF THE HEART	$4.99 U.S.	☐
	by Miranda Jarrett	$5.99 CAN.	☐

(limited quantities available on certain titles)

TOTAL AMOUNT		$ _____
DEDUCT: 10% DISCOUNT FOR 2+ BOOKS		$ _____
POSTAGE & HANDLING		$ _____
($1.00 for one book, 50¢ for each additional)		
APPLICABLE TAXES*		$ _____
TOTAL PAYABLE		$ _____

(check or money order—please do not send cash)

To order, complete this form and send it, along with a check or money order for the total above, payable to Harlequin Books, to: **In the U.S.:** 3010 Walden Avenue, P.O. Box 9047, Buffalo, NY 14269-9047; **In Canada:** P.O. Box 613, Fort Erie, Ontario, L2A 5X3.

Name: _____

Address: _____ City: _____

State/Prov.: _____ Zip/Postal Code: _____

*New York residents remit applicable sales taxes.
Canadian residents remit applicable GST and provincial taxes.

Look us up on-line at: http://www.romance.net

HBKOD97

Harlequin Romance®
and Harlequin Presents®

bring you two great new miniseries with one thing in common—MEN! They're sexy, successful and available!

You won't want to miss these exciting romances
by some of your favorite authors,
written from the male point of view.

Harlequin Romance® brings you

Starting in January 1998 with Rebecca Winters,
we'll be bringing you one **Bachelor Territory** book
every other month. Look for books by Val Daniels,
Emma Richmond, Lucy Gordon, Heather Allison
and Barbara McMahon.

Harlequin Presents® launches **MAN TALK**
in April 1998 with bestselling author Charlotte Lamb.
Watch for books by Alison Kelly, Sandra Field and
Emma Darcy in June, August and October 1998.

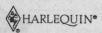 HARLEQUIN® *There are two sides to every story...
and now it's his turn!*